IMPERFECT ILLUSIONS

C. A. HOLLISTER

CONTENTS

CHAPTER 1

VALERIE

VAL PACED THE LENGTH of the sidewalk in front of the rustic restaurant, its inviting glow seeping out from the large windows. A cool mid-April breeze nipped at her skin, causing a slight shiver she tried to dismiss as she walked. The aroma of roasting garlic and simmering herbs wafted from the kitchen vent, mingling with the earthy scent of the rain-soaked pavement.

The soft, rhythmic sound of her heels hitting the cement walkway echoed the pounding of her anxious heart. She heard the faint buzz of conversation and laughter spilling out every time the door opened, briefly melding with the soft jazz melody floating in the background.

Her hands twisted at her midsection, crumpling the delicate fabric of her dress. It offered little comfort as her stomach churned with an unsettling mixture of unease and nausea.

"It's just a date," she whispered to herself, trying to soothe her frazzled nerves, but her voice trembled with the weight of anxiety.

This date was a stupid idea. She only agreed to it because Lisa wouldn't stop badgering her to get out of the apartment and join the real world again. But Val was very much in the real world. Every day, she went to work and interacted with the public. Her job was selling dream vacations to weary people, desperate to get away.

"You need to get laid," Lisa blurted out one night while they were enjoying a few too many beers at the local sports bar around the corner of Val's apartment. "It's been what, seven months since you and Thomas broke up?"

"Six," Val corrected, well aware how pathetic it was to be counting the days since her life had been mangled into something unrecognizable.

Val didn't need to get laid. She didn't need a date. She needed answers. Why did Thomas throw away two years of their lives for another woman? If he was so unhappy, why didn't he tell her sooner? She supported him through every setback, every success, both good and bad. Still, it wasn't good enough.

"Valerie?"

The invocation of her name snapped Val out of her circling thoughts. She spun around, her hair swaying slightly, sending a subtle whiff of her floral perfume into the air. A man stood a few feet away, his presence like a solid anchor in her sea of swirling anxiety.

His cautious smile deepened, a dimple in his left cheek softening the sharp lines of his clean-shaven jaw. The faint glow of the streetlamp highlighted the hazel depths of his eyes, which held a mixture of curiosity and confidence.

"I'm Wayne," he said, his voice calming her frazzled nerves, yet the proximity to this stranger amplified her reservations.

Val mentally shook herself. "Valerie. Val. Call me Val," she stammered, her voice a mix of hesitation and a desperate attempt at normalcy. Get it together, woman, she admonished to herself.

His smile widened, deepening the dimple. "Our table is ready."

For a second, she thought about telling him she changed her mind. That she made a mistake by accepting the date. Knowing Lisa would never let her live it down if she did, Val attempted a shy smile before walking through the door he held open, careful to keep her distance.

Inside, he led her across the room to a secluded corner, where a small table with two empty wine glasses waited. "I wasn't sure what you wanted to drink."

"And here I thought chivalry was a thing of the past." As soon as she spoke, more embarrassment heated her neck and face.

Wayne sat in the chair across from her, waving down a waiter. His smile stayed in place when he said, "I'm trying to bring it back into fashion."

The waiter came to their table and after another long awkward argument with herself, Val decided on a glass of wine. "Something dark and tart."

"Good call." To the waiter, Wayne said, "We will have the Malbec." When they were alone, Wayne settled those intense eyes on her, sending a flutter of nerves throughout her stomach. "I hope you don't mind, but I wanted to learn a little about you before our date. Lisa gave me a few conversation starters."

Brushing more hair behind her ear, Val said, "As long as she left a little mystery to be had. A girl needs her secrets."

His laughter sounded like honey to her ears, thick and rich. "Don't we all."

They shared a long minute of silence. The surrounding tables became an echo chamber of clinking cutlery and half heard conversations. The couple to the left leaned into each other, and if one didn't look too closely, they might appear to be having an intimate conversation.

But Val noticed the way the woman's stare narrowed on him, using her pointer finger to tap the table with each hushed whisper hissing out of her painted lips. The man kept his eyes focused on the empty plate before him. Tight lines framed his mouth, and the hand resting on the table squeezed tight around a white cloth napkin. That couple used to be her and Thomas. Talking past each other until there was nothing else to say.

Wayne cleared his throat and said, "So, you work at a travel agency? That must come with some marvelous perks."

Val turned away from the other couple, mortified she had lost herself in people watching instead of being present in the moment. Pulling her napkin in her lap, she twisted the fabric to help soothe her nerves. "It's not as lucrative and exciting as it sounds, though you're right. It does come with some nice discounts."

"I wish I had more time to do my own thing, but work keeps me tied down."

"I know what you mean." The segue in the conversation further loosened the tightness in her muscles. "Don't get me wrong, I'd love to take off for a weekend here and there, but life hasn't exactly presented me with many opportunities. Lately, I've been so—" She stopped herself from blurting out the taboo subject of her love life. "I've been busy with other things."

The waiter brought their drinks, and she had to make a conscious effort not to gulp hers down. After a dainty sip, she set the delicate stemmed glass on the table. In her head, she searched for anything to say to at least pretend to add something to the conversation. "Lisa mentioned you are a photographer. You shot her cousin's wedding last year, I think?"

He relaxed into the chair, his features pensive for a second before smiling again. Damn, he had a beautiful smile. "Daniel and Melissa. The venue was phenomenal. It made for gorgeous photographs."

"I heard the ceremony was one of a kind. I wish I could have gone."

"Oh? Why didn't you go?"

She stared into the depth of her wine glass. "Personal reasons."

Their conversation fell into another awkward lull. Val's attention started to wander toward the couple, still engrossed in their argument, but she mentally shook herself, keeping her focus on the table. Their uncomfortable silence was interrupted by the waiter.

"Have you decided on an entrée?"

Wayne grabbed the menu resting on the edge of the table. "I guess we forgot to look it over."

Val was relieved to see the hint of red flush his cheeks. At least she wasn't the only awkward one on their date.

He nodded to Val's menu. "The duck is out of this world."

Not having much of an appetite, she said, "Sounds good. The duck it is."

When they were alone again, she noted the way he bounced a finger on the cream-colored tablecloth. After a few more seconds of silence, Wayne said, "Lisa mentioned you are an artist."

She meant to laugh off the comment, but it came out as a snort, and her face grew warm again. "Hardly. It's just something to pass the time. I like to sketch landscapes, mostly. A lot of people only see the surface. I want to push past the veil and admire the true beauty that lies beneath." Inside, she groaned at herself to shut up already. But she couldn't help it. She rambled when nervous.

"I feel the same way." He leaned forward, and inexplicably, her pulse quickened. "That's what I love about weddings. Everyone is put together so perfectly, but if you know what you're looking for, it's easy to find the real people behind all that makeup and fancy clothes." To her surprise, he reached out and rested his hand on hers. "I wish I had my camera. You look stunning in this light."

She managed not to yank her hand away, instead, slid it into her lap. Her gaze dropped to the empty space in front of her. "Dim lights and harsh shadows can do wonders for a girl."

"You would look gorgeous in any lighting."

When she looked up, his eyes trapped her in their depths. It would have been easy to pass off his comment as some cheesy pick up line, but the sincerity she saw in his stare was real. The waiter saved her from giddy laughter, ready to bubble out of her by refilling their drinks.

Wayne leaned back, his gaze sliding to the side before settling back on her. "Have you ever visited Utah?"

Thankful for the change in subject, she relaxed. "Like I said, I don't get much time to myself. I haven't left New Mexico in a couple of years."

"Well, if you get the chance, you should visit the Highland Ridge Resort. The mountains are breathtaking this time of year."

"Oh, where is it located?"

"A quaint town called River Pass. My family used to vacation at the resort all the time. In fact, my sister chose the location for her wedding because of the view of the mountains." The tightness in his face softened as he reminisced. "I used to love visiting that place. To get away from everything and simply be." He looked past her, as if recalling a memory, but he quickly reined himself in. This time, his smile didn't quite reach his eyes.

"Wow, it sounds beautiful. If I ever have the opportunity, I will definitely check it out."

By the time their main course arrived, the conversation had settled into an easy rhythm, the initial awkwardness fading like the background jazz wafting through the restaurant. Val launched into a couple of anecdotes about her more difficult clients, painting vivid pictures of their outrageous demands.

"One woman called me five times in one afternoon to ask if the resort had gluten-free shampoo in the rooms," she said, rolling her eye. "When I told her no, she actually asked if I could 'pull some strings.'" She made air quotes with her fingers. "Because, obviously, I have so much sway over shampoo suppliers halfway across the world."

Wayne snorted into his wine glass, trying not to laugh too loud. "Please tell me you told her you'd have the CEO of Gluten-Free Suds on the next flight."

"I wish! Instead, I spent thirty minutes trying to explain that shampoo isn't meant to be eaten." She shook her head, her laughter tinged with exasperation. "The next day, she canceled the entire trip. Said it was a 'health hazard.'"

Wayne leaned back in his chair, chuckling. "That's nothing. I once photographed a wedding where the groom caught the bride making out with his cousin—during the reception." He shook his head in mock disbelief. "The fight that broke out was like something out of a wrestling match. Tables flipped, the cake hit the floor, and—of course—the cops showed up."

Val gasped, her hand flying to her mouth. "You're kidding!"

"Not even a little. The best part? The cousin apologized to me for ruining my shoot as he was being handcuffed. Priorities, I guess."

Their shared laughter drew the attention of a few nearby diners, but neither seemed to notice. Somehow, the conversation shifted to food and cooking. Val reluctantly admitted, "I have the culinary skills of a college freshman. Most of my meals come in a box or a bag. If it requires more than boiling water, I'm out."

Wayne smirked, raising a brow. "You mean to tell me you've never tried your hand at anything gourmet? Ever?"

"Once," she admitted with a grimace, disbelieving she was actually telling him the story. "It ended with a smoke alarm, a ruined lasagna, and Lisa banning me from her kitchen."

"Tragic." He nodded solemnly, then added, "Though I can't judge. My skills pretty much stop at grilling a decent steak. But I can bake a damn delicious potato."

Val tilted her head. "A baked potato? That's your claim to culinary fame?"

"Hey, don't knock it until you've tried it," he said, holding up a hand. "I'm talking crispy skin, perfectly seasoned, sour cream, butter, bacon, chives—the works."

Her eyes narrowed playfully. "Okay, but can you do it without setting off a fire alarm?"

Wayne tapped his chin, pretending to think. "Now that you mention it, my smoke detector did sing me a little song the last time I made one."

"That's comforting," she quipped, shaking her head. "So, we're both hopeless."

"Hopeless and proud," he agreed, lifting his wine glass for a toast.

Val clinked her glass against his, her earlier nerves a distant memory. "To takeout and box meals, then."

"And perfectly baked potatoes," he added with a wink.

When it came time for the date to end, she chewed at her lower lip, disappointed it was over. Not that she would tell Lisa about their wonderful date. That would leave the door open to another blind date. Although Val wasn't opposed to Wayne asking her out again. Maybe that's why she stayed in her seat long after their dishes were cleared away.

She stared at the check next to him, calculating her part of the meal. She got as far as reaching into her clutch when he said, "Dinner is on me."

"I don't mind paying my share."

He flashed one of those knee melting smile, and she found herself grinning back. "I insist," he said with a wink.

When the waiter returned with Wayne's credit card, she glanced around the room, then her to her watch. "I guess we should go. It's getting late."

Wayne stood, helping Val out of the chair, showing the same chivalry as before. Outside, the wind had picked up, bringing with it the faint hint of rain.

"Thank you for the lovely evening," he said, taking a step toward her. The breeze carried the scent of his cologne, and she wasn't sure if he noticed the shudder that passed over her. His faint smile never wavered. "I had a wonderful time."

"Me too." The honesty of it surprised her, and she found herself smiling.

He held her gaze when he leaned in. Her whole body went stiff. Countless reasons to stop him circled her thoughts, but it took only one tiny voice in the back of her mind to silence the rest. She eased forward. The kiss was brief but electric, leaving her breathless.

He pulled back, his lips barely touching hers. "Would you like to come home with me?"

A simple, direct question, deserving of a simple, direct answer. Of course, she wouldn't go home with him. They just met. She wasn't the type of person to entertain one-night stands. Staring into his eyes, Val acknowledged the silly idea that maybe this date wouldn't be the last.

She opened her mouth to tell him she was flattered, but her voice couldn't get past her throat. It was a single night. A chance to feel something real after her world fell apart. Squeezing his hands, she said, "Okay."

His smile felt good against her lips when he kissed her again. "Where are you parked?"

She took a few seconds to reel in her racing thoughts and pointed across the street to her Nissan.

"I'll bring my car around and you can follow me." When he crossed the street, he kept glancing behind him, as if making sure she still waited for him and not running for the hills. Seeing his own nervous behavior somehow put her more at ease.

By the time she got behind the wheel, her heart pounded more so from anxiety than excitement. The sensible woman that had carved a path out of her small-town life demanded she drive away immediately and forget about this perfect date with this gorgeous man that ticked all the right boxes in all the right ways.

Yet the flustered, lonely woman who spent the last six months pining for a dead relationship demanded she have this single night of wonderful promises. She owed herself one memory untainted by loss or regret.

A dark blue Audi pulled up beside her. Wayne motioned from the driver's seat for her to roll down the window. "My apartment isn't far from here."

All she could do was nod and force her expression to soften. "Lead the way."

CHAPTER 2

WAYNE

WAYNE DROVE THROUGH THE quiet, lamp-lit streets, the buzz of the evening settling into something deeper and more magnetic as he approached his apartment complex. For most of the drive, his mind focused on the look on Val's face as they stood on the sidewalk—the flicker of nerves mixed with something daring, like she was on the edge of a decision that could tip either way. Relief flooded through him when she said yes, and it surprised him.

As he pulled into the gated entrance of his complex, he kept glancing in the rearview mirror, expecting Val to change her mind and drive past. When she followed him into the parking lot and the gate slid closed, the finality of it sent a flutter of nerves shuddering through him. A sensation he wasn't used to feeling.

Normally, he shoved his emotions to the back of his mind. But with Valerie, everything was different. Her genuine demeanor was refreshing. The attraction he felt for her was foreign to him. It wasn't just her timeless beauty that caught his eye. Her sincerity eased him into letting down his guard and open up to her. Nights like this were usually filled with meaningless talk. An appetizer to the inevitability of the evening.

He backed his car into his assigned spot and hurried to direct Val to the space across from his building reserved for guests. She hesitated in her seat, a hand reaching into her purse, as if searching for something. Courage maybe? Or an excuse to leave. His heart dipping unexpectedly. Part of him almost wanted her to go, to spare him the regret that would come when he was alone again. He tamped down the feeling, stepping forward and tapping gently on her window.

Her eyes snapped up to his, then her expression hardened into determination, and she opened the door and stepped out, clutching her purse like a shield.

"My apartment is on the second floor," he said, offering her a small, reassuring smile he hoped would ease the tension radiating from her.

Maybe it was the fear she might bolt to her car and drive away that made him slip his hand into hers. A heartbeat of hesitation passed, but she didn't pull back like she did in the restaurant.

On the landing, she stopped, and her fingers trembled slightly. "I don't normally do this," she admitted, voice low, eyes focused on the faded cement of the breezeway. "I'm not the type of girl who follows a virtual stranger to his place with the expectation of—"

Wayne stepped closer, gently tilting her chin upward. "I didn't invite you here for sex. I enjoyed our evening, and I don't want it to end."

She raised a brow, skepticism flashing across her face. "Sex was implied. Especially after that kiss."

Her bluntness drew a soft laugh from him, the tension between them loosening slightly. "I'd be lying if I said I wasn't attracted to you, but you're in charge tonight. Whatever you decide, I'll respect it."

His words seemed to steady her, and she followed him into his apartment, clutching her purse close. Her gaze wandered over the simple space—the clean lines of the furniture, the neutral tones, the absence of clutter. To the outside observer, it probably seemed impersonal, almost like a carefully curated exhibit. To Wayne, it's the order he needed in his life to feel like he had some kind of control over his future.

Her face didn't give away what she might be thinking, but her demeanor further relaxed, and she dropped her hands to her waist, still clutching the purse. He was hit with the overwhelming urge to impress her, to show her more of himself, beyond the night's flirtations. Then again, he took an enormous leap, inviting her into his home. He'd book them a room in the hotel across from the restaurant. He should have taken them there.

Pushing past his own discomfort, he walked to the short bar separating the living room and the kitchen slash dining room to where he kept an assortment of liquor. "Would you like a drink?"

She shook her head. "No, thanks. The wine from dinner is still doing its job." Her smile wavered before falling away again. He got the feeling she was still processing her decision to come here. He came back to the living room empty-handed and sat down on the couch.

Instead of joining him, Val wandered the room, pausing in front of the photos on his walls. "Is this your family?" she asked, her voice softening.

"Yeah, those are my parents," he said, noticing how she studied their faces as if searching for pieces of him in their features. He moved to stand beside her. "And that's my sister." He gestured to another picture, this one of him and his sister on a beach, both smiling at the camera with sunlit waves in the background.

"She's beautiful." Looking over more photos, she asked, "Is she your only sibling?"

He nodded, glancing at the photo, memories stirring in his chest. He liked the way she spoke to him, as if he was more than a simple distraction for the night.

Returning to the couch, he patted the cushion beside him. After a moment, she joined him, though her posture remained tense.

"What about you? Do you have family nearby?" His questions surprised him. Usually, the women in his life didn't care about small talk, but Val genuinely seemed interested in him, and he wanted to show her the same courtesy.

The way her mouth worked up into an embarrassed smile sent a shiver down his spine. "No, they live in Texas. I moved away as soon as I graduated from high school. But I visit them on holidays."

"Any brothers or sisters?" Why did he keep asking her stupid questions that didn't matter?

"An older brother. He was nearly twelve by the time I came along." Her smile bloomed, as did the rush of pink in her cheeks. "He always called me a midlife crisis baby. But he's a good big brother. We just aren't that close, given the age gap."

The room filled with silence, and it stretched to the point of being uncomfortable.

"Do you have any photo shoots coming up?" she asked, shattering the quiet.

"Not for a few months. I offered to photograph my sister's wedding, but she turned me down. Said she wanted me as her best man, not a photographer." He chuckled, and her lips curved into a faint smile, though her attention still seemed distant.

She dropped her head for a moment, before shifting her stare back to him. There was a question in her eyes, a silent plea for reassurance. When he reached for her hand, her hesitation melted. She leaned forward, her breath brushing against his cheek before their lips met. Their kiss started slow, tentative, until he felt her surrender to the moment, and he deepened the kiss, guiding her with gentle certainty.

He rose from the couch, his hand never leaving hers as he led her down the hallway, every step marking a silent agreement between them. When he opened the door to his bedroom, her gaze settled on the bed, reservations slipping away. His own resolve faltered. Was this really what he wanted? Their night had been perfect, almost magical. He wouldn't regret it if tonight together ended with a kiss.

Whatever thoughts had been at the forefront of his mind slipped away when they crossed the threshold into his sanctuary.

This was her choice, and for the first time in a long while, it was his choice, too.

CHAPTER 3

VALERIE

THE MODEST SIZED BEDROOM lay before her, neat and well put together as the rest of the apartment. When they broke from their embrace, Wayne stepped away from her, backing toward the queen size bed. His simple tastes were reflected in the solid maroon comforter and matching pillowcases.

Val's pulse raced with an excitement she hadn't experienced in a long time. The room faded around her, leaving only the bed and Wayne. His lips parted into a sensual smile, making her heart hammer that much harder in her chest.

He extended an arm. "Come here." His voice called to her like a siren's song, both beautiful and commanding. She moved across the plush carpet to meet him at the bed. His fingers traced the contours of her torso and waist. His touch, no longer gentle, gripped her hips and spun her around. Had it not been for one of his arms anchored around her waist, she would have fallen forward onto the comforter from the momentum.

Her throat squeezed shut, locking her voice behind the anticipation of what was about to happen. Jumbled thoughts darted in sporadic directions, matching the erratic beating of her heart. Her pulse rushed through her ears, drowning out her rasping breath.

By the time she came back to reality again, her dress draped over her lower body. He swept her hair away from her neck and each kiss he laid on her exposed shoulder made it harder for her to take in air until she thought she was going to suffocate from the sheer force of her desire.

Given her meager cup size, she had no need for a bra, giving him one less barrier to traverse. Standing in only a pair of dark green silk panties, she fought the uncomfortable surge of embarrassment heating her skin at the thought of him judging her too thin frame and lack of curves.

Whatever insecurities trying to bully their way into the forefront of her mind quickly vanished when a hand came around to cup one of her breasts, squeezing as he rocked forward. His erection pressed into her, accompanied by a low rumble vibrating against her back.

He slipped inside her underwear, gentle and teasing. If she was able to form actual words, she would have begged him to push a little deeper so he could reach a part of her that ached for release. He eased his hand free and bent her over the bed, working her panties down her legs and up under her knees. The unexpected sensation of his tongue made her yelp and fall forward onto her face.

She rolled over, expecting him to laugh, or say something pointed about how silly she was behaving. Instead, he took in her body with a simmering, hungry stare, matching his smile. Her mouth dropped open, ready to apologize for being so weird. That would undoubtedly lead to a flood of incoherent babbling about how this was the first time she'd been with a man since her break up, and Thomas hadn't been so incredibly sensual in their love making.

Wayne climbed on top of her before she said any of those things. He hovered over her mouth, his gaze searching both her face and eyes. A flash of something she couldn't quite name passed over his features. His kiss banished the last of her inhibitions. The weight of his body settled onto her, drawing another hungry moan, and she urged him deeper into the embrace. Shaking fingers fumbled with his shirt, and he moved away, giving her room to reach his buttons, but the damn things kept slipping out of her grasp.

He got to his knees to help. Instead of returning to their kiss, he began an exquisite exploration, starting at her neck and a painfully slow continuation down her breasts, then her stomach, easing downward until he reached her thighs. His breath was hot against her bare skin. She worked her fingers into his hair in anticipation.

Val didn't expect to orgasm so quickly, but what his tongue demanded she was helpless to deny. Hundreds of thousands of bolts of lightning exploded outward to every nerve of her body. The air crackled with the electricity and her voice filled the small space between them. Incoherent syllables and half-finished thoughts escaped her parted lips. His hands latched onto her legs, refusing to let her slip away as she bucked and writhed against him.

After what seemed like an eternity, she came back to herself, clinging to him, her chest heaving. He began the slow ascent up her belly, pausing at each breast and teasing her nipples with his teeth.

She sat up, urging him to the edge of the bed. The timid woman who followed him home was satisfied, leaving only desire and need in her wake. Val's fingers were no longer trembling when she undid his pants, pushing them down to the floor. The black boxers he wore bulged where his erection pushed at the seam. When there was no longer clothing impeding her reach, she took him into her hand, squeezing as she worked her fingers up the length of him.

He shivered and went to move her back onto the bed, but a woman she didn't recognize smacked his hands away.

"What are you doing?" His words were nearly as breathless as she felt. "You don't have to—"

She cut her eyes upward. "I'm in control, remember?" The force of her voice surprised her, but she ignored both his shocked expression and her own insecurity.

Her mouth enveloped him, reveling in the taste. Her thoughts swirled with how foreign it was to be so in control. No one else had ever made her yearn to give the same kinds of pleasure he showed her.

After only a short time, he slipped out of her grasp, almost tripping over his pants still around his ankles. He reached down and for a tense moment, she thought he was going to pull up his jeans and walk out.

Instead, he kicked out of his shoes and finished undressing.

"Sorry," she said. "I haven't had a lot of practice with—you know." She waved a hand at his midsection.

His smile wasn't malicious, but eager. "You were about to make me embarrass myself."

She bit at her lower lip. "Oh."

Reaching for the nightstand, he pulled out a silver wrapped condom. "I think we've had enough foreplay."

Whatever tenderness he'd shown before disappeared when he climbed on top of her again. His movements were made with a need of his own and she welcomed the force with which he pushed inside her. He went deeper with each stroke, drawing her ever closer to another glorious release. She arched into the climax, crying out with each throbbing pulse.

Her world spun as he rolled over, bringing her up with him. He clung to her, his kiss demanding more. She thought she would dissipate into the very air when she came again. Beneath her, Wayne shuddered when he joined her through that fall into bliss. Yet he didn't stop her from taking every last ounce of ecstasy. She fell onto the bed beside him, sated and panting.

When her breath slowed and she could form coherent words again, she said, "Oh my God, that was—wow."

The bed shook with his laughter. "Yes, definitely wow."

Another minute went by and she maneuvered to her side. "Can I ask a favor?"

His brows furrowed, his grin wary. "What kind of favor?"

"Don't tell Lisa about this. If she finds out I had such a good time, she's going to try to set me up again." His relaxed grin faded, and he took on a perplexed expression, so she added, "I'm not saying I'm opposed to another date. You're easy to talk to and we seem to have a lot in common."

When his confusion deepened, she sat all the way up, her skin tingling with embarrassment. In her head, she yelled at herself to stop talking. "I'm not getting all weird and clingy. I totally get it. This was meant to be a onetime thing. Lisa told me you are moving soon to work on your portfolio, but we can have some fun before you leave. I mean, it's completely up to you." God, why couldn't she be quiet?

He sat up so fast, she had to lean back to keep from being knocked over. "Why would she say that? I'm not going anywhere. Didn't she tell you about the date?"

It was her turn to be confused. Awkwardness shifted into. "What are you talking about? You mean the date we just went on?" The post orgasm calm gave way to a clammy gnawing in her gut.

He scooted off the bed and gathered their clothes. "I don't think it's a good idea to see each other again."

Val clamped down on the humiliation working up her body. "Right. Of course." She got to her feet, snatching the dress from his hand. It took every ounce of will power to keep her emotions from bursting through the forced calm she clung to.

Wayne stopped dressing and tried to pull her face toward him, but she jerked away, sidestepping his touch. "It's not what you think," he said.

"Look, I'm fully aware of what tonight is supposed to be."

"No, Val, I don't think you are. I had an amazing time with you, and I'm not referring to the sex. The whole evening was—" When he refused to continue the thought, she slipped the dress over her head, finally meeting his stare.

"It's fine." It wasn't even close to being fine, but all she wanted to do was get away from him, away from the apartment. "I'm sure Lisa filled you in on my pitiful story and you did this as a favor or something."

"What? No. That's not what tonight—" His body deflated. "Jesus, I can't believe she didn't tell you."

The desperation in his voice made her turn all the way around to face him. "Tell me what?"

"You should ask her."

Frustrated, she took a step toward him. "You're here now, so tell me what the fuck is going on? You say you enjoyed the date, but now it's suddenly not a good idea to go out again? If you want this to be a one-night stand, then tell me."

His gaze kept slipping past hers. When he finally looked her in the eye, regret stared back. "It's true. Lisa and I met at the wedding. I must have given her the wrong card. She called me a few days ago to set everything up. The date. The time. The restaurant. She paid for everything."

Val blinked past the shock holding her still. "I'm sorry. Did you say she paid you? Actual money to go out with me? To sleep with me?"

He snatched his jeans upward. "Lisa told me to treat tonight like the real thing. It was your choice how the night ended."

Val's stomach knotted and her skin went clammy. It had felt real. And that's what hurt her so deeply. God, she was such a fool. The bedroom that had been comforting moments before now seemed sterile and staged. "Everything you said, the photography, your love of art—it was a lie?"

"No. I never lied about any of it. But photography doesn't pay the bills, so I have this gig on the side."

The way he passed off his sex work as a gig made another wave of nausea run through her. She covered her face and let out a groan. "This can't be happening."

"I thought you knew."

She shook her head and went back to dressing. How had she let herself get to the point where her best friend thought she had to pay someone to go out with her? Val had been so lost in her own misery, Lisa felt the need to save her from herself.

Raw emotions blurred her vision. One of the last things Thomas said to her before he left was how unsatisfied he'd been with her, both in the bedroom and on an intellectual level. He'd basically told her she didn't give him the level of intimacy he needed.

"I am so sorry." Wayne reached out, but she jerked away and rushed to the living room, snatching her purse off the couch.

She hesitated when she saw the pepper spray but reached past it to her wallet and took out a twenty-dollar bill. "I'm not sure what the proper tip should be. I hope this is enough."

He refused to take the money, so she threw it on the floor.

"Please, don't leave like this." Wayne's voice was faint and echoed the pain in her chest.

She hesitated, her hand tightening on the knob. The sight of the money reminded her of the perfect evening with the perfect man. And it was all a paid for experience.

Her footsteps echoed down the stairs. At her car, she fumbled in her purse to grab her keys, her fingers refusing to push the damn unlock button. Rain pelted the top of her head, adding to the urgency of her movements. Before she pulled away, she glimpsed Wayne's outline standing at the top of the stairs, and a fresh wave of humility washed over her.

CHAPTER 4

WAYNE

WAYNE STOOD MOTIONLESS IN the silence of the apartment. He came back in to grab his keys and go after Valerie, but that would only make things worse. The fragrance of her sweet perfume still lingered in the air and its presence clashed with the cold reality of her abrupt departure.

He moved to the window, following the taillights of Val's car as they disappeared into the night. A deep void settled in his chest that was a stark reminder of the empty space his profession had carved inside him. He had grown accustomed to the transient nature of his encounters that left no lasting mark. Usually, he shrugged off the loneliness. He had to compartmentalize his life to avoid feeling anything real. But with Val, the barren sensation was more like a hollow ache. Her tilted smile and warm laughter had penetrated his well-crafted facade.

As he stood alone in his apartment, wallowing in the harsh reality that came from a near perfect night, his cellphone rang, breaking the silence. He saw the name lighting up the display and hesitated for a moment before answering.

"Hey, Sheila."

"Did I catch you at a bad time?"

He forced a lightness into his voice he didn't feel. "Not at all. What's up?"

"It's about the wedding," she began, her tone a mix of excitement and stress. "I need your opinion on something."

Wayne listened, half-distracted by his own thoughts.

"I'm trying to come up with a fun night for both the boys and girls to enjoy together. Neither Paul nor I are keen on the whole bachelor and bachelorette party idea."

"Why not plan a dinner and show in Salt Lake."

"That's the problem. Apparently, Daddy has arranged for the family to attend a ballet on Thursday. I don't want to torture you boys with two shows in one week. Didn't you and Rita have a couple's weekend in Salt Lake before—"

His already sour mood darkened. It had been months since he thought about Rita. The love he used to feel for her had withered from regret to a stale anger. He obsessed for months over why she'd cut all contact with him after her last goodbye text. Now, he found he didn't care why anymore. Whatever her reason for leaving, it no longer mattered. He turned toward the door, regretting his choice to not go after Val.

"You still there?"

Running his fingers through his hair, he said, "We could go to Nicolina's. It's a rooftop bar downtown. They host local bands from time to time."

"That's perfect. I'll have Paul make a reservation. Hopefully, it's not too late." She paused. "Are you sure you're okay? You sound off."

"I'm good." He looked around his neatly arranged apartment, a space mirroring his life—orderly, controlled, but devoid of genuine warmth. A harsh but short-lived bolt of jealousy ran through him. He envied his sister and the love she had found, despite their strained family dynamics. She was lucky enough to break free of a lifetime of unrealistic expectations, whereas Wayne was doomed to be a product of those strict guidelines.

"Can I ask you something?" he said.

"Sure."

He took a few seconds to compose his question. "How did you know Paul was the one? I mean, you and I haven't exactly had the best role models when it comes to love. What swept you off your feet?"

Sheila paused, considering his question. "It's hard to say, exactly. One day, I knew he was my forever."

"So, it wasn't love at first sight?"

"Heck no," she giggled. "The first time I met him, I thought I was way out of his league. Snobbish of me, I know, but Paul persisted. Why are you suddenly curious about my relationship?" She sucked in a breath. "Has my baby brother met someone?"

"No," he said too quickly, then thought of Val, her laughter, her unguarded moments, the way she looked at him with a mixture of curiosity and longing.

Sheila let the silence between them grow until it became uncomfortable.

"Maybe." He ran a hand down his face. "It's complicated." Wayne's eyes went to the twenty-dollar bill still lying on the floor. Shame flared inside his chest, and he had the sudden need to lash out, but kept his composure while still on the phone.

"Okay, well, I'll have plenty of time to grill you next week."

"Can't wait."

After the call ended, Wayne sat in the dim light of his living room, staring at the sterile space. The conversation with his sister lingered in his mind. Sheila found something genuine, something lasting. And for a brief moment, he had glimpsed a similar possibility—a chance at a connection that went beyond the transactional nature of his work.

He replayed the evening with Val, each moment a vivid memory. Her initial nervousness, the way she had leaned into him, her presence filling his apartment, the softness of her skin under his touch. It had all seemed so real, so right. But the reality of who he was; what he'd done lay between them like an insurmountable barrier.

Wayne knew he had to make a choice. He could continue down the path he had chosen, a path of fleeting encounters and empty connections, or take a risk, and chase something like what he had felt with Val.

Who was he kidding? After what happened, she would never believe a word that came out of his mouth. And he couldn't blame her. What would he say if he called her? What could he possibly say to change her perception of him?

He went to his room and stared at the mass of blankets and sheets wadded up at the end of the bed. Having his space in such disarray would normally drive him crazy, but he couldn't bring himself to strip the bed. Val had been the first woman he invited back to his place. Letting her into his personal space had been a momentary lapse in judgment on his part. One he couldn't afford to make again.

Resigned to the cold hard truth that he missed out on an amazing woman, he started to mentally prepare himself for his sister's upcoming nuptials and the prospect of dealing with his family.

CHAPTER 5

VALERIE

DAYBREAK CAME AND WENT, sending light sneaking through the blinds in stubborn streaks. But Val ignored it all. Curled up in her bed, she clung to the shadows as if they could shield her from the reality of going home with a complete stranger. The opportunity for her to break out of the self-induced prison of her past turned into a humiliating reminder of just how pathetic her life had become.

The incessant knocking at the door finally tore her from the cocoon of her sheets. She knew it was Lisa. The barrage of calls and texts had been coming in all morning. Maybe ignoring them wasn't a good idea.

Dragging herself out of bed, Val shuffled past the dress crumpled on the floor beside the dresser, fighting off a fresh pang of tears. She flung open the door to find Lisa there, her expression morphing from relief to worry in an instant.

"Hey. Are you okay? I tried calling like a million times."

"I'm fine," Val replied, her voice thick with an edge, hinting she was anything but okay.

"You don't look fine." Lisa's brow furrowed as she stepped past Val, despite the arm barring her way. "What happened? Was the date that bad?"

Val's stare remained fixed on the floor. "It was quite good, actually. Wayne was great. Perfect, even." She lifted her eyes. "And the sex," she paused, "out of this world."

Lisa's eyebrow arched, skepticism painting her features. "Okay. So why the sour mood? I thought you'd be glowing."

"I know the truth."

Lisa exhaled a soft, "Oh."

"Oh? You pay someone to go out with me, and all you can say is 'oh'?"

"Val, you've sulked around this apartment for months."

Val cut her off with renewed anger in her stare. "You didn't warn me or anything. You let me go on the date thinking it was real."

"Because I knew you wouldn't go if I told you the truth. You've been shutting yourself off from the world for months. I wanted you to remember what it's like to be happy again."

"Happy? You think paying someone to pretend to care about me is going to make me happy? Do you have any idea how humiliated I was when I found out the truth about him?"

"It wasn't like that. I thought—"

"You thought what? That I'd never find out? I wouldn't care? God, Lisa, you don't get it. You made me feel like I'm so pathetic I can't find a date on my own."

"I'm trying to help you move on." Lisa's attempt to justify her actions stumbled into silence as the gravity of her mistake settled between them.

"If you really wanted to help, you could have supported me through this terrible time in my life."

"That's what I've been doing. For months, now. What Thomas did to you was horrible, but my God, Val, you need to let him go. He's not worth the agony you're putting yourself through."

The two women stared at each other for a long time, neither knowing what else to say. Finally, Val walked past her friend, and when she reached the kitchen, she paused. All she wanted to do was scream, to say something unforgivable, but four years of friendship kept her from lashing out. "I don't want to be around you right now."

Lisa took in a breath, her pain visible in the way her lips quivered. "Come on, you don't mean that."

"What you did—It's no better than Thomas cheating on me."

The hurt pinching her friend's features made Val's chest tighten. "That's not fair," Lisa whispered.

Val closed her eyes, pushing tears onto her cheeks. "I need some time to think about things."

Before walking out, Lisa looked over her shoulder and said, "If you need anything, call me, okay?"

Val had to bite her tongue to keep from asking her to stay, but the pain was too fresh. "Sure."

Alone, Val bypassed the kitchenette and sank into the chair at her computer desk. The quiet hum of the machine was a stark contrast to the turmoil inside her. During the long, terrible hours she lay in bed, alone with her thoughts, she kicked around the idea of getting away. Lisa suggested a vacation and now it didn't sound so bad.

The logo of her travel agency blinked at her from the screen like a beacon of escape. She made a quick detour to her bank's website to check her savings. Any grand ideas of getting away faded when she saw the puny three-digit number staring back at her. Her attention veered away from the desktop to the open doorway of her room.

Sitting in the jewelry box on top of her chest of drawers was the engagement ring Thomas bought her, where it had been since the day they broke up. She had every intention of giving it back, but they never reconnected after she kicked him out. The thought of selling it felt like severing the last thread of their life together. A final goodbye. And maybe that's what she needed.

The money she would get from the ring would be more than enough for a vacation. Thomas bragged about the price to anyone who would listen. It wasn't the hope diamond or anything, but if she sold it for half of what he paid, she would have plenty of disposable income to play with.

Before she talked herself out of it, she navigated to the employee log in page of the travel agency where she worked. From there, she typed in a destination she had in mind and calculated the price, including her discount. A week-long vacation away from her job, her life and the people in it was just what she needed to clear her head.

It pained her to pull out the credit card she kept locked away for dire emergencies, but she didn't want to wait for a jeweler to appraise the ring and haggle over the price. She'd worry about that when she returned.

Packing turned into a mechanical process, her hands moving with a certainty her heart lacked. The scent of lavender from her clothes mingled with the mustiness of the hot pink suitcase, a bittersweet reminder of the getaway she and Thomas had planned as a first real vacation as a couple. They poured over brochures for weeks, circling destinations, planning itineraries. For two years, he promised to take her somewhere amazing. But the trip never came.

The call to her boss had gone better than expected, despite how busy they were. Val told Donna of the three weeks she was owed, Val was only asking for one. That alone spoke volumes about the mental state Val was in, willing to burn her world to the ground to have a few precious days away.

The far-off sounds of the city served as a reminder to Val, as she loaded her car, of what she was leaving, filling her with a mixture of fear and anticipation. She couldn't remember the last time she'd traveled overnight on her own. She prided herself on her independence, but somewhere along the way, she fell back into old habits of depending on others for her own happiness. This vacation was a chance to rediscover herself and the woman she set out to become when she left Texas and her family behind.

CHAPTER 6

WAYNE

THE NUMBERS ON THE digital screen of the gas pump ticked upward in sluggish increments, the mechanical whir a hollow echo in the quiet lot. Wayne rested a forearm against the top of the pump, gaze drifting past the service road to the interstate beyond. The afternoon sun cast a molten shimmer over the asphalt, making the endless stream of cars appear like mirages in the heat. For two days, he'd been running on autopilot, stretching the drive out longer than necessary, postponing the inevitable.

He'd told himself that leaving a day early would keep him from feeling rushed, but in truth, it had only given him more time to think. Too much time. Every mile behind him felt like a tether he'd been unraveling, but instead of relief, all he found was the gnawing ache of regret.

New Mexico still called to him. No. Not the place. It was the loose thread of unfinished business he'd left behind. Val.

His fingers twitched against his phone, the phantom memory of an unsent message prickling in his mind. Halfway through the drive, he'd pulled into a rest stop, thumb hovering over Lisa's contact. At first, he'd wanted to send a tirade, demanding to know why she'd put Val in such an impossible position. Then, the anger burned off, leaving only the quieter, more desperate impulse. He wanted to ask for Val's number. Reach out, fix what had gone wrong.

He'd typed the message. Then deleted it. Typed another. Deleted that one too.

In the end, he shoved his phone into the cupholder and sat in silence, staring at his own reflection in the rearview mirror. When he got back, he'd send Lisa her money—every damn cent. Along with an extra twenty for the 'tip' Val had thrown at him like he was worth nothing more than a passing transaction. It stung more than it should have. But he couldn't blame her. He'd made his choices.

With a sigh, Wayne glanced at the pump. The numbers crawled upward at an agonizing pace, and his patience wore thinner by the second. If he left now, he'd have enough gas to reach the resort. But there was no hurry. Another two minutes wouldn't change anything.

The parking lot stretched around him, empty save for a pair of semi-trucks idling near the convenience store, their drivers nowhere in sight. He envied them—their freedom, their distance from expectation. He wondered what his life would look like if he'd chosen differently. If he'd walked away from his family's plans back in college, pursued something; anything else.

A flicker of movement caught his attention. The glint of sunlight bouncing off a car's windshield, a sleek sedan creeping forward in the stalled traffic. His pulse stuttered.

The color, the make, the model—identical to Val's.

He straightened, eyes locked onto the vehicle, heart hammering as he tried to make out the driver. The glare off the glass obscured their face, but he thought, just for a second, he saw a silhouette of a woman behind the wheel.

The air in his lungs went sharp and shallow.

Val?

His body tensed with the irrational urge to move, to get closer, to confirm what his heart already knew wasn't possible. But just as quickly as the moment came, it slipped away. The car inched forward, lost among the others as traffic picked up speed. Reality settled like a weight on his chest.

Not her.

It wasn't her.

With a muttered curse, he wrenched his attention back to the pump, his frustration bubbling over. He didn't have the patience for this. Yanking the nozzle free, he shoved it back into place, leaving the tank half-filled. Enough to get where he was going. That was all that mattered.

In the driver's seat, he pulled out his phone, the screen lighting up with a new text from an unfamiliar number.

Hey, are you available?

Wayne exhaled through his nose, rubbing a hand over his jaw. The message was simple, routine—just another client looking for a carefully manufactured illusion. A fleeting moment of attention.

For years, that had been enough for him. He had mastered the art of being whatever a woman wanted him to be. Attentive. Charming. A fantasy wrapped in real flesh and blood. And he had been paid well for it.

But now?

Now, all he could think about was Val—how she'd seen through the mask he wore for everyone else. How, for the first time in as long as he could remember, he'd felt real.

His thumbs hovered over the keyboard before he finally typed out a response.

Out of town.

The three little dots appeared almost instantly. Then, a second later, a sad-face emoji.

A humorless chuckle escaped him. The irony wasn't lost on him. Wayne McNabb, professional lady's man, leaving women feeling special for a living, yet utterly failing when it came to the only woman who mattered.

With a shake of his head, he tossed his phone onto the passenger seat and pulled onto the service road. Up ahead, the traffic had cleared, the slow crawl replaced with a steady stream of movement. He merged onto the interstate, fingers tightening on the wheel as the gas station shrank in his rearview.

Two more hours. Then he could disappear into his hotel room, away from the memories clawing at his thoughts. Away from everything.

He reached for the radio, flipping through stations until a familiar melody filled the car. A love song—one he had heard a hundred times but had never truly listened to.

Now, though? Now, the lyrics hit a little too close.

With a quiet sigh, Wayne kept driving.

CHAPTER 7

VALERIE

VAL FLIPPED DOWN THE visor, blocking out the afternoon sun from her tired eyes. Her hopes of making the fourteen hour drive in one day had been over zealous on her part, made even more impossible when she found herself with a flat tire after four hours on the road. The extra expense of a new tire and a motel room made a hefty dent in her budget, but she refused to turn back. She booked the perfect resort in the perfect location promising a full week of pampering, posh amenities and hiking trails touting phenomenal views. She wouldn't get another chance like this again for a long time.

The longer the drive went on, the more guilt ate at her for how she left things with Lisa. Every stop she made, Val pulled out her phone to send an apology text. Then she remembered the humiliation that came with Lisa's attempt to 'make her happy'.

Val didn't know what was more embarrassing. The blind date with a male escort, her decision to go home with him, or that her best friend thought it necessary to intervene in her love life to such a drastic degree. All three scenarios were equally mortifying.

Spending so much time alone in the car made her confront parts of herself she had been hiding from for the last year. Her relationship with Thomas had been over for a long time before he cheated. She just didn't want to admit it to herself. She had grown too comfortable in the life they created, so she ignored the warning signs until she couldn't anymore.

Part of her knew she had been playing the victim these last few months in a desperate attempt to keep from having to face the reality of what her life had become. And it was light years away from the one she envisioned when she left home at eighteen, determined to make her mark on the world with her art.

Before the breakup, she kept pretending the woman she saw in the mirror every day wasn't getting more and more unrecognizable. When Thomas moved out, she realized he had been slowly and carefully chipping away at her self esteem, molding her into the person he wanted her to be. In the end, he still chose to toss her aside for someone else, like she was some failed experiment.

After the date with Wayne, she embraced the anger sliding into her heart where love used to be. Yet through all the pain and heartache he put her through, a weak, pathetic part of herself still held out hope that Thomas would come crawling back. Then she could humiliate him like he did her.

What Lisa did was a foolish attempt to give Val back the dignity and independence he took away.

A sign up ahead announced her arrival to Silverlake, distracting her from the loneliness in the car. She sat up straighter in the driver's seat, searching for the exit, taking her to the resort. The prospect of getting out of the cramped space made her heart race. She planned to spend the rest of the night soaking in the tub and lounging around the room. Tomorrow, she'd explore the mountain trail within walking distance of the resort. After that, she didn't have any concrete plans. This week was her chance to find some semblance of the old Valerie.

A six-story building came into view over the next hill. It's rustic, yet modern architecture silhouetted by mountains and the fading afternoon sun. She pulled under the awning and a young man greeted her with a warm smile. He looked like he still belonged in high school. Dark blue eyes complemented his cherub face.

"Good afternoon, Ma'am." He held the driver's door while she got out.

When he went to climb in, she said, "Oh, I have some bags in the back."

"I'll grab them for you."

She hesitated at the rotating doors. A childhood memory of her cousin's broken hand caused a momentary shiver. Opting for the safety of the regular entrance, she stepped into the lobby, her eyes immediately drawn upward. The ceiling boasted exposed wooden beams, adding a rustic charm to the modern decor.

Sunlight filtered through large windows, illuminating the lobby with a warm, natural glow. The floors were a mix of rugged stone and polished wood, and along the walls, historical photographs of the area added a touch of local heritage. At the center, a modest stone fountain burbled, its water echoing softly in the spacious room, instantly soothing her nerves.

Guests chatted near a large seating area. A wooden reception desk, manned by a friendly-faced concierge, offered pamphlets on local attractions and trail maps.

She stepped up to the stone counter running the length of one wall. A middle-aged woman dressed in a dark pants suit gave her best customer service smile. "Hello. How can I help you?"

Val's attention went to the gold name plate on her lapel. Margie. "I have a reservation. Valerie Peters."

Margie looked down, her fingers flying across the keyboard. "Did you say Peters?"

"Yes."

Her manicured brows stitched together as she frowned. "I don't see your name in our system. Did someone else make the reservation for you?"

"No. I booked it myself a couple of days ago."

Pushing a confident customer service smile back onto her tinted lips, she said, "No worries. Let me check something else."

The sound of clacking heels distracted Val from the panic easing into her chest. Out of her periphery, she saw a woman fast walking toward the entrance.

She squealed with delight, her voice bouncing off the high ceiling. "There you are."

Val eased her eyes to the side, trying not to look obvious about eavesdropping. For a terrifying few seconds, she thought she was hallucinating. She watched in utter disbelief as Wayne pulled the woman into a hug. This had to be a mirage. The long drive scrambled her brain. Surely, the universe wasn't cruel enough to put Wayne in the same resort on the same day. And on one of his infamous 'dates'?

"Miss Peters."

The sound of her name cut through the shock, but she couldn't make herself turn away from the scene behind her.

"Ma'am."

"Yeah," came Val's distracted reply.

"I'm sorry, but you don't have a reservation with us. At all."

Val tore herself away from Wayne, giving Margie her full attention. "What? That can't be right. I got a confirmation email."

"And you're sure it was for this week?"

"Yes." Val took out her phone and showed Margie the email.

"I don't understand. We've been booked solid for months."

Val heard the clicking of the other woman's heels getting closer, her voice quieter now. "When you called earlier and said you were going to be late, Paul wondered if you were trying to back out."

Wayne's laughter sent a tingling sensation down her spine, remembering how it sounded next to her ear. "Come on, Sheila, you know I wouldn't miss your wedding for the world."

His statement left Val even more confused, though she felt a sense of relief knowing he was off the clock. Then she remembered their conversation about the wedding. He hadn't mentioned specific dates, but if she'd known this was the venue, she would have postponed her vacation or chosen a different place altogether.

"I'm glad you're here," his sister said. "Jennifer has been unbearable. She's trying to hijack my big day. Come on. Dads with Paul at the bar."

Wayne looked from his sister to where Val stood gawking at him. His expression shifted into the same look of shock she imagined was plastered all over her face. "I'm pretty beat," he managed through his surprise. "I think I'm going to head up to my room before dinner."

"Oh no you don't. You're not leaving me to deal with your mother."

"I promise I'll be around to run interference, but right now I don't have the fortitude for her."

"Miss Peters?"

Val spun back to Margie, eyes wide.

"I see what happened. Our system should have blocked out these dates. I'm not quite sure how you booked them in the first place."

Val's mouth dropped open, unsure of how to respond. Her first instinct was to get angry at the concierge, but it wasn't her fault the resort's computer system had a faulty booking system. Fighting to keep her road weary emotions under control, she said, "I don't have anywhere else to go."

Margie turned her attention back to the monitor. "There's a nice hotel in Chandler. It's about seventeen miles north of here. I can make some calls. See if they have something available."

Before Val could answer, Wayne sidled up to the counter. He tried to make eye contact, but she refused to give him the satisfaction.

"There you are." A woman who shared his sun-kissed complexion and sharp features approached the desk.

Wayne turned and gave her a brief hug. "Hey, Mom."

"Sheila said you were going to your room. Why don't you join us for a cocktail before dinner."

"I'm beat. I'll see you later tonight."

"Did you come alone?" His mom glanced around the lobby, purposefully overlooking Val. He didn't have a chance to answer before she went on. "Excellent. When I heard about poor Abigale,

I suggested Rita take her place. I always thought you two made the perfect couple."

"Mom—"

With the finesse of a woman used to getting her way, she cut him off. "Also, your Uncle Jarod will be here this evening. He's been hinting he needs someone to take over one of his stores in Nevada."

"We've been over this. I have my hands full with my photography."

"You can do that anywhere. You need a career that pays a living wage. Not some hobby."

"It's not a hobby. I'm doing quite well for myself. Besides, I have other sources of income."

Val snorted and immediately turned away, pretending not to be listening to their conversation. After a few seconds, she felt their stares boring into the back of her head. When she looked to the side, Wayne's eyes were wide and pleading.

His mother gave Val a once over. "Are you two acquainted?"

"Yes," he blurted out.

Val snapped her mouth shut, cutting off her reply.

He moved closer to her and said, "Mom, I'd like you to meet my date, Valerie."

His mother's scrutinizing gaze intensified. "You didn't mention a plus one."

His expression shifted to frustration. "Can we not do this now? It's been a long drive."

She waved off her son and took Val's hand. "Wayne has a bad habit of not telling his family anything. It's a pleasure to meet you, Valerie. I'm sorry if I seemed rude." She gave Wayne a narrowed glare that wasn't quite gone when she returned to Val. "I look forward to learning more about you."

Before Val could reciprocate, his mother was already walking away.

When they were alone, Val turned on Wayne. "What the hell?" she hissed.

"I don't know. I panicked."

"Panicked? You just lied to your mom about me being your date."

As if waiting for the right opportunity, the clerk said, "I'm sorry. There's nothing available in Chandler either. You can try Salt Lake."

Val ignored the hammering of her heart and the dejected look on Wayne's face, and walked to where her luggage waited on a bell hop. If she ended up making the drive to Salk Lake, she couldn't afford anything as fancy as the resort. But a seedy motel would be preferable to the prospect of getting back on the road.

Wayne appeared at her side, keeping a respectable distance. "I may have a solution to your problem."

"And what would that be?"

"What if I let you stay with me? In my room."

A bolt of heat ran up her neck and face. "Absolutely not. Not only is your room the last place I'd want to be, but I refuse to be a scapegoat for whatever family drama you've got going on. Besides, I think your mom is hoping to fix you up with that Rita woman."

He stepped between her and her luggage. "That's never going to happen."

Val crossed her arms, curious enough to wonder about their history, but nowhere near brave enough to ask.

He must have seen the curiosity on her face because after a few seconds of silence, he said, "She's my ex. It's a long story, but after she broke it off I—It's the reason I chose the—It's why I'm in the business I'm in."

Val rolled her eyes. "Oh right. Like your life is so horrible pleasuring all those women."

His already dour demeanor darkened. "You have no idea what it's like to be in my shoes."

"But I know what it's like to be in your bed." She went around him, grabbing her bags. "Good luck with your family."

"I wasn't the one who set you up on the date. Stop blaming me for what's out of my control."

She scowled at his back as he stomped away. How dare he bring up the obvious? It didn't matter if he had been oblivious to her ignorance. Just thinking about their night together made her skin burn with shame. She had been the one to accept his proposal to go back to his place.

Burying the guilt swirling inside her chest, she went to one of the tall picture windows facing a beautiful mountain scape. The view reminded her of what she would be missing if she went back home.

Running into Wayne in such a random location was bad enough. To consider sharing a room with him was unbelievably stupid. Dangerous, even. He had been paid to be her ideal date. Whatever attraction she felt for him was based on lies. It didn't quell the pathetic longing, giving her a sliver of hope that maybe some of what he said had been true.

Everything came down to one simple fact. She didn't have the money to spend on an alternate solution. If she demanded a refund on the reservation, it would take time to be put back on her card. And time was not something she had a lot of. Not when she planned for a week of self reflection in one of the most beautiful locations she'd ever seen.

Val studied the lobby, taking in its warmth and charm. She and Wayne were grown adults. They were perfectly capable of setting hard boundaries and expectations that were mutually beneficial to them both.

A high-pitched whine accompanied her footsteps as she turned on her heels and set her bags on the luggage rack next to the elevators. She caught Margie looking at her on the way by and fought back another surge of embarrassment.

CHAPTER 8

WAYNE

WAYNE'S MIND REELED AT the sudden appearance of Valerie. Since their date three nights ago, her face haunted his thoughts and dreams. For a brief moment, he entertained the idea that maybe his desires had somehow manifested in some magical way to bring her back into his life. It was a silly, nonsensical thing to believe. Yet, he couldn't deny the excitement quickly following the shock of seeing her in person again.

Then she had the serendipitous mishap of her reservation being overbooked. He hadn't fully thought out the suggestion for her to stay in his room before blurting it out. The desperation to shield himself from his overbearing mother had compounded the urge to redeem himself with Val. He needed to tell her how terrible he felt about deceiving her, although it wasn't his fault. The vehemence of her refusal stung more than it should have.

A voice in the back of his mind, the one that allowed him to endure the life he'd been living the last nine months, piped up and asked him why he cared in the first place. Valerie Peters was simply one more body in the long line of women in his short-lived career. What was so special about her?

He couldn't answer the question right away. Val had been the one constant in his thoughts and daydreams over the last few days. To have her appear in his life in such a random way couldn't be mere coincidence. Could it?

Wayne spotted his dad standing near the bar, talking to Paul. Sheila made her way across the room, joining her friends. Sometimes Wayne felt jealous of his sister and how easily she opened herself up to others. The few times he'd tried to emulate her lifestyle, he'd been hurt and betrayed. Rita was the catalyst leading to the wall he put up around himself and his heart. Not since she left him had he let anyone inside.

Despite his best efforts, Wayne failed to hide the sour expression pulling at his features. He tried to relax the muscles in his face, but it was too late. His dad had an uncanny ability to see right through most any guise.

"Got yourself into trouble already?"

Wayne smiled at the flippant way his dad pretended not to dig for information, yet making light of a potentially terrible situation. "Have you seen Mom? I need to talk to her."

His dad scanned the room. "She's around here somewhere, scouting potential clients, I imagine. I swear that woman never stops working." He looked at Wayne again. "Is everything alright?"

"Yeah."

"You have the same look on your face as when you broke your grandmother's urn."

"Nothing like that." It's worse, he thought to himself.

Before he could go on, a familiar set of fingers slipped around his left bicep. He looked to the side to find Val standing there, the anger gone from her features.

She barely made eye contact with him before saying, "Sorry to keep you waiting. It took me a while to navigate this place."

Wayne stared at her delicate hand, amazed at how such a light grip could feel so powerful. He carefully eased out of her grasp, sliding her hand down to her side. Her eyes flicked downward, but when she lifted them again, she wore a halfway convincing smile.

"You must be Wayne's father. I'm Valerie. It's nice to meet you, Mr. McNab."

His dad's face betrayed his confusion, but his smile was genuine. "It's very good to meet you as well, Valerie. Call me Greg." To Wayne he said, "You didn't tell me you were bringing a date."

"It was a last-minute decision." Val interjected. "We haven't been dating very long, and I wasn't sure if it would be appropriate to just show up since I've yet to meet the family."

His dad's smile widened. "You are most welcome, my dear."

Wayne held out his arm beside her, careful not to make contact. "I'm going to take Valerie to our room so we can change before dinner."

"I thought you were looking for your mother."

"It can wait."

When they were in the lobby and out of eyesight, Wayne spun around. "What are you doing?"

"Honestly, I have no idea. I guess I need this vacation more than I don't want to be here with you."

He ran a hand down his face. The day-old stubble he'd been too lazy to shave tickled his palm. "This will never work. I'm sorry I even suggested it."

Her demeanor shifted. It was like watching the same transformation come over her when she found out the truth about him.

The tightening around her eyes and mouth was followed by a sharp, "Fine. I thought I'd do you a favor. Good luck with explaining why you lied about me."

He didn't give her a chance to walk away before reaching for her arm, letting go almost as soon as he touched her. "What do you want in return?"

Her body relaxed, and he had to fight off a smile at the way her eyes narrowed and her mouth puckered in thought.

"I have certain things I want to do while I'm here, and I'd like to stick to my itinerary without being glued to your hip the whole time. You are free to do whatever you want with whomever you want."

Her last comment wiped any traces of amusement from his face. "That's not why I'm here."

She shrugged. "You never know when a good business opportunity will turn up."

"Are you offering to pay for those services?"

Her mouth fell open slightly, and she shifted her stance from one foot to the other before her expression solidified into irritation. "I've tasted the forbidden fruit. It's overrated."

Amused by her quick wit, he replied, "One thing I've learned in my short time in this business is how to gauge just how satisfied a woman is at the end of our night together. I more than earned my money with you."

Surprise flashed through her eyes, which she quickly hid behind a frown. "Don't flatter yourself. I hadn't been with a man in a very long time. Any sex not involving silicone and batteries would have gotten the same results." She spun on her heels and headed for the elevator without giving him a chance to respond.

Maybe he should be insulted by the way she spoke to him, but he was more concerned with the dangerous feelings her cheeky comments invoked. His pulse pounded in his ears from both excitement and anxiety. He wanted nothing more than to take her upstairs and revisit their first night together. His fingertips tingled with the memory of the satin feel of her skin.

"You coming?" Val stood inside the elevator, holding a hand over the door to keep it from closing. "Or are you going to stand in the lobby and sulk all afternoon?"

At least his desire didn't show. He pushed a neutral expression on his face and joined her in the elevator. "Six," he said, nodding to the numbered pad next to her.

Already, he was regretting his decision.

CHAPTER 9

VALERIE

Neither Val nor Wayne spoke for the entire ride to the sixth floor. The space between them was chilled with an icy silence that persisted even when they were walking down the hall. At one point, she realized she had taken the lead and had no idea which room they were staying in. She slowed her pace, letting Wayne walk ahead.

He pushed open the door to their room. She had to clamp her mouth shut, so it didn't hang open as she marveled at the opulent decor. When she booked her stay, her room had been on the first floor, and she was pretty sure it wasn't near as grand as this one.

The entryway was softly lit, touched by the rich scent of polished wood and something floral and fresh. The room beyond was larger and grander than she'd imagined, with a muted elegance making her instantly conscious of the scuff on her suitcase and the worn strap of her shoulder bag.

The spacious living area sprawled out before her, grounded by wide, deep-brown hardwood floors and an intricate rug in earthy tones appearing both ancient and impossibly soft. A plush taupe-colored sofa sat invitingly across from it, piled with small, square pillows in shades of gray and green that echoed the nearby mountains she could see through a wall of windows. Floor-to-ceiling glass framed an astonishing view: dark green pines fading into the distance, with the Wasatch Mountains rising bold and jagged behind them, their tips dusted with a light veil of snow. A set of heavy glass doors led to a private balcony, and she could almost feel the clean mountain air pulling her outside.

To her left was a gourmet kitchenette she wouldn't dare use, not with its marble counters and gleaming appliances that looked like they belonged in a magazine. The fridge and cabinets blended seamlessly into the dark wood, too elegant to be interrupted by labels or handles. A breakfast bar with polished leather stools separated the kitchen from the living area, somehow managing to look sleek and rustic at the same time.

And then, in the center of it all, was a small wooden dining table beneath a modern chandelier. The glossy dark table was clearly made from something expensive, with four leather-backed chairs around it—way more space than she'd ever need, but the kind of luxurious "just because" extra that seemed to be everywhere in this suite.

"The bedroom is through there." Wayne pointed to a framed doorway near a set of curtained doors. "The room has one bathroom. It's connected to the master suite and the living space, so knock before you barge in."

She turned back to land on Wayne. "Have you been in this room before?"

He looked over the open space. "I don't think I've stayed in this particular room, but the layout is similar to others on this floor."

She recalled him mentioning how he and his family used to vacation here when he was younger. A cynical voice in her head whispered questions, curious about the possibility of him bringing other women to the resort. Pushing the line of thought to the far reaches her mind, she went to the bedroom to unpack.

Beyond the curtained door, she caught a glimpse of a small terrace with two cushioned chairs overlooking a spectacular view of the mountains. She could see herself lounging out there, losing herself in her sketchbook.

Val hesitated in the doorway of the bedroom, letting the details sink in. The space was quiet and softly lit, with an atmosphere that felt almost reverent, almost too perfect to disturb.

A king-sized bed dominated the room, draped in layers of soft gray linens that looked like they'd been ironed into place by some unseen hand. The duvet was thick and inviting, with a subtle sheen catching the low, golden light from a set of wall sconces on either side of the bed. A mountain of plush pillows in the same shades of silver, charcoal, and white as the living room were stacked in precise layers, and she almost felt guilty at the thought of disturbing them. It was the kind of bed she could melt into.

For a fleeting moment, the room seemed like a sanctuary, a soft and beautiful escape from everything outside its doors.

Glancing at the suitcase in her hand, she realized she didn't belong in this world. The stark contrast of hot pink to the elegance of the soft gray comforter was stark and jarring. Pushing past her insecurities, she set the suitcase gently on the bed and opened it up.

The bed bounced when Wayne flopped his luggage beside hers. The deep mahogany leather matched the simple aesthetic of his apartment. He grabbed a couple of items of clothing and put them into the chest of drawers across from the bed.

"What do you think you're doing?"

Without looking at her, he said, "Unpacking. There are hangers in the closet if you want to do the same."

She blocked his path to the bed. "I hope you don't think you're sleeping in here."

"Of course I am. It's my room."

"No, it's our room and I'm laying claim to nice, comfy the bed. There's a big couch in the other room with your name all over it."

He stared at her, and she could practically hear the cogs in his caveman brain spinning. She crossed her arms. "I'm doing you a favor. The least you can do is offer the bed to your date."

"Girlfriend," he corrected. "You made that clear when you introduced yourself to my dad. And it's big enough for the both of us. I don't bite." He inched closer to her. "Unless you ask nicely."

She swallowed involuntarily, then spit out a disgusted sound and pointed to the bedroom door. "Couch."

With a roll of his eyes, he continued to unpack. "You can at least share the drawer space."

He picked out a dark polo shirt and matching jeans and headed for the door. "Dinner is at six."

As soon as the door closed, she went to the bed. She studied the multitude of colorful tops and sundresses she'd hastily packed before leaving for Utah. There was no rhyme or reason to her wardrobe. This weekend was supposed to be relaxing, where she got to do whatever she wanted with no expectation of uptight dinners with strangers.

She picked up a floral, knee length dress, pleated at the waistline. It was a favorite of hers because it gave the illusion she had actual curves on her twiggy frame. She made a mental note to follow through with the gym membership idea Lisa kept suggesting. Maybe if she toned her body, she wouldn't need the magic of push-up bras and curve building clothing.

Given the muted color option Wayne chose, she wondered if the outfit would be too loud and casual for the occasion. Dress still in hand, she opened the bedroom door to ask Wayne his opinion about the outfit. She stopped mid-stride when she walked out to find him pulling down a pair of maroon silk boxers and caught an eye full of his naked midsection. Even flaccid, he was impressive.

She threw herself behind the safety of the door. Heat crept up her neck, and she willed herself not to look again. But the image of his bare skin lingered. She tried to banish the flutter stirring low in her stomach. She was here for space, not distractions.

"Why are you naked?" Her voice betrayed the shock of seeing him in the nude again.

He paused, then he said, "How else am I supposed to change clothes?"

"You couldn't do that in the bathroom?"

"I thought you were in there already. Why are you being so weird? It's not like we haven't seen each other's most intimate naughty bits."

"That's not the point. Next time, change in the bathroom like a civilized human being."

"Sure, whatever."

As she went to close the door, she remembered why she went out there in the first place. After a quick peek to make sure he was decent, she held up the dress. "Do you think this will be okay for dinner?"

He barely glanced up as he buttoned his jeans. "Should be."

"Is there a dress code?"

He threw on the polo and went to the kitchenette, where he grabbed a bottle of water from the fridge. "Not that I'm aware of. I'm sure whatever you have will be fine."

"Yeah, but won't we clash?"

After a long swallow, he turned his full attention to her and the dress. "I think no one will care."

"You're no help."

He shrugged, taking another sip.

Unimpressed with his lack of enthusiasm, she returned to the bedroom, her irritation lingering as she got ready. By the time she finished dressing, she almost canceled on him. A quick knock sounded at the door. Wayne's voice called, "It's almost six."

When she stepped out, she caught his brief, surprised look. But he quickly recovered, giving her a nod before heading for the door. He murmured, "Let's get this over with," but she didn't miss the faint smile that tugged at his lips.

In the elevator, Val said, "We should get our story straight." She stared at her reflection in the mirrored surface of the elevator, making sure her attention didn't wander to the man beside her.

"What story?"

"Our fake relationship. Every woman in the room is going to want details."

The bell dinged, and the doors opened, revealing a nearly deserted lobby. Wayne held out his arm for her to exit the elevator first. At least he was still chivalrous.

On their way to the restaurant, he sidled up to her left side. "Keep it simple. I don't want a lot of unimportant details to remember."

Val gave him a snarky grin. "I'll tell them I got tricked into being one of your tricks."

He frowned. "My family doesn't know about that part of my life. I'd like to keep that way. You're not going to make me feel bad for my choices."

"If you're so content with what you do, then it shouldn't be a big deal if your family knows the truth about you."

Seeing the shift from anger to dread and back to anger again made her look away and study the intricate details of the filigree adorning the walls. "I won't breathe a word. We have an agreement, remember?"

"Thank you."

She followed Wayne as they weaved through halls and came to a restaurant on far side of the resort. The group of people waiting made her anxiety skyrocket, and she threw herself to one side. "I can't do this."

His gaze flicked from the doors to her. "What do you mean, you can't do this? It's a little late to back out now."

She stared at him, her racing heart making it hard to concentrate on coherent words. "What if I say the wrong thing? Your mom seems like the type of person to have me arrested for fraud or something."

He sighed, taking hold of her hand. The warmth of his fingers stirred an unwanted shiver up her spine. "Calm down. You'll be fine. It's just dinner. Everyone is going to be so fixated on Sheila's wedding, they won't even notice our presence." He let her go and added, "Besides, Mom isn't the type to call the cops. She has other ways of making problems go away."

Val's anxiety doubled until she saw the glint of humor in his snarky grin. "Not funny."

He held out his hand. "Shall we?"

There were only two more chairs left at the long table, which made them the last to arrive for dinner, so all eyes were on the young couple when they sat down. Wayne put Val beside his sister while he sat next to an older man sharing some of Wayne's features, except the other man's eyes were a light shade of blue.

"You must be Valerie," his sister said with a conspiratorial smile.

"That would be me." Val rubbed a hand down the back of her neck, trying to tamp down her anxiety.

"I'm Sheila." Smiling at Wayne, she added, "So this is the someone you avoided talking about on the phone?"

Val turned a curious stare on him, unsure of what to make of the question, but Wayne refused to meet her stare. Instead, he grabbed the glass of water in front of him.

Needing to fill the awkward silence, Val said, "Well, we haven't been dating for long. It's been a whirlwind romance."

"That's so sweet." Sheila leaned forward. "How did you two meet?"

Val felt Wayne shift beside her, but ignored the unspoken warning. "It's a funny story, actually." She paused, taking her own sip of water, wishing for something a little stronger. "He photographed a friend's wedding. I had a little too much to drink on an empty stomach and about the time I got on the dance floor, I forgot how gravity worked. If not for Wayne, I would have fallen flat on my face."

Sheila smiled. "A regular knight in shining armor."

Val looked over at Wayne, his brow lifting as if to accuse her of over sharing. His smile seemed less forced, but still tight. "I saw a beautiful woman in need of help," he said.

"This photography thing is really worth your time, then?" Jennifer's comment drew Val's attention to the other side of the table.

His mother kept her eyes locked on Val, even though she was talking to Wayne.

"He's following his passion." Sheila's tone was firm, making her words clipped.

"Passion doesn't pay the bills." Jennifer said, smiling. At least it was supposed to be a smile, but on that woman, it looked more like a cat assessing its prey. "I'm sure you understand the need to prioritize duty over a hobby, don't you, Valerie?"

Val put her hands in her lap, so everyone couldn't see her twisting the napkin. Sharing the same love of art as Wayne, she understood his desire to have the freedom to pursue his art. "Sure, a career is important, but who's to say you can't make a career out of something you love?" Even if the job entailed lots of hot, steamy sex with random strangers for money.

"You're okay with supporting the both of you while Wayne chases his dreams?"

"She doesn't support me," Wayne interjected. "I make a good living on my own."

Greg lifted a hand, flagging down one of the wait staff. "I'm starving. Why don't we order our meal now?"

The unspoken request to drop the subject led others around the table to start their own conversations. Val was relieved to have their attention off her and the nonexistent relationship she had with Wayne. And she was especially thankful for the champagne that arrived soon after.

As her attention wandered from one conversation to another, Val couldn't help but feel like a spectator, caught between Jennifer's judgmental looks and Sheila's easy warmth. The way the family bantered so openly was foreign to her. Val's mom and dad were more reserved, comfortable with silence and distance. Certain things were simply not aired in public.

Eventually, Val came around to Greg and Paul in a heated debate about a recent trade involving one of her favorite baseball teams. She jumped into their conversation without thinking. "An absurd move on the owner's part."

Paul eyed her, sipping at the dark lager beer in his hand. "You follow baseball?"

The sudden attention made her reach for her glass for a quick sip. "I'm no fanatic, but I frequent the bar at the end of my block."

Greg asked, "What's your take on the whole ordeal?"

"Timing is everything, isn't it? Shipping off their star pitcher right after the All-Star break. With the playoffs on the horizon, it feels like they're throwing in the towel too early. Anyone paying attention would raise an eyebrow."

Paul nudged his soon to be father-in-law. "See, I told you something was off."

Sheila waved a hand. "Alright, no more baseball talk at the table, or you three can take it to the bar and debate there."

Greg put on an exaggerated frown. "You're no fun, pumpkin."

For the rest of the meal, Val made a point of blending into the background, embarrassed she had called so much attention to herself. Wayne didn't exactly ignore her, but his time was being monopolized by the man she assumed to be the uncle Jennifer mentioned earlier. He kept insisting Wayne would love the change of scenery when he moved to Nevada. Maybe Val should encourage Wayne to take the job. It would get him out of her life for good.

By the end of the night, she'd learned more about the McNab family than she knew about most of her own. It was a surreal experience to be around people who talked so openly about themselves. Her parents made a sport of pirouetting around meaningful conversation.

Sheila sought Val out while everyone meandered away from the table. "Would you like to join the girls and I for a night cap? It will give us some time to get to know each other before the wedding."

Val shot a quick glance at Wayne, who said, "It's been a long day for us. We're beat."

Wayne held on to Val's hand on the way to the elevator. As soon as the doors closed, he let go and leaned against the back wall. She could feel his stare on the back of her head.

"What?" she asked, finally.

"I'm going to have to bring you to all my family functions. My dad is absolutely smitten."

Crossing her arms, she said, "You wanted me to fit in, so that's what I did."

"What was with that story of how we met?"

Pretending to be picking at some lint on her dress, she said, "I attended a wedding a few years ago. Unfortunately, no one saved me from the humiliating fall. I'm sure someone has a photo floating around of me on the ground, holding a napkin to a bloodied nose." She left out the part where she'd met Thomas that same night due to the mishap. She had been rushing to the bathroom and nearly mowed him over. It turned out he was attending a conference in the same hotel.

Wayne's laughter snatched her out of the memory. "If I had been there, I'd like to think I would have tried to save you."

The bell announced their arrival, and she rushed out of the elevator and down the hall to their door, only to have to wait for him to reach her. When he got the door open, she said, "I'm going to need my own key."

He handed it to her. "I'll grab another one tomorrow."

"Thanks."

CHAPTER 10

WAYNE

WAYNE STARED AFTER VAL until she disappeared into the bedroom, listening for the click of the lock on the bathroom door. Instead of pulling out the hide-a-bed, he stepped onto the narrow balcony and breathed in the warm, dry air. A hint of rain lingered on the lazy breeze sweeping through the valley. Above, the stars twinkled in and out of sight between thin clouds obscuring their light.

His mind wandered to the dinner, and the way Val had effortlessly navigated his family. Especially his mom. He found it nearly impossible to keep from staring at Val all night. Not only because of her beauty, but in the back of his mind, he worried she really would slip up and say something to would expose them both.

Trying to lead a double life, given his family's high-profile lifestyle, wore on him. It was the main reason he chose to move so far away, where no one knew him or his last name.

Still, there was always the fear of the next woman he 'dated' would connect him back to his family. He had been so careful to never divulge too much about himself. Not even his full name. But people were keyboard sleuths nowadays and one innocent search could expose everything. It was yet another reason he shouldn't have brought Val to his apartment.

The lock on the door to the bathroom clicked again, and he heard the other door open and close in the bedroom. He took the opportunity to jump into the shower. It took a concentrated effort not to think about Val as he washed.

The dress she chose clung to her curves, highlighting every delicious detail of the body he knew lay underneath. She'd put her hair in a loose updo that framed her face in a way to highlight her toffy colored eyes. The lip gloss she wore accentuated the perfect cupid's bow of her lips, and he wanted so badly to kiss them again. But it was her perfume that drove him to the point of madness. Every time he caught a whiff of her delicate rose scent, it quickened his pulse.

No one affected him like she did, and his attraction went beyond the physical. Not even Rita had excited him so intensely.

By the time he finished with his shower, Wayne had a hard time coaxing down the erection, making it difficult to dry off and dress. He certainly didn't want to walk out of the bathroom and have Val seeing the truth of his feelings he had for her. When he saw she wasn't in the living room, he went to the couch. He was unhappy about being kicked out of the comfortable bed, yet at the same time, relieved that he wasn't put in a tempting situation.

He'd just gotten under the covers, ready to settle into his book, when the bedroom door opened. Val stepped out wearing a thin spaghetti strapped night shirt and matching cotton shorts. Her loosed hair fell over her shoulders. Every step she took sent a hint of her shampoo into the air. He moved the book downward to hide the raised blanket over his groin.

She made her way to the kitchenette, barely looking in his direction, and grabbed a water bottle from the fridge, but hesitated. It occurred to Wayne that even though they knew so little about each other, he could practically hear the internal struggle inside her mind about the cost of a single bottle of water.

He saw her getting ready to put it back and said, "It's free." He was lying, of course. But he wasn't going to let something like a two-dollar water dampen her stay.

She stared at him over her shoulder, her eyes narrowed in suspicion. After a few seconds, she closed the fridge and headed back to the bedroom, water in hand. On the way by, he noticed her gaze linger on the book in his lap, making him wonder if it was the words on the paperback grabbing her attention, or the thought of what lay hidden beneath.

"Is it any good?"

The question nearly made him laugh. Had he not been so unsure of his own feelings, he might have made some snarky comment reminding her of the other night. Instead, he lifted the book a couple of inches off the blanket, making sure it still hid the seemingly ever-present erection. "I don't know yet. I'm still on chapter one."

"It's on my list. After the other dozen or so books I don't have time to read."

"I haven't really gotten into it yet. You can have it if you want."

Her smile made his mouth go dry. She nodded to the bedroom door. "I'm already invested in the book I brought, but thanks for the offer."

He sat forward when she started to walk away. "Hey."

She glanced over her shoulder, hand resting on the knob.

For an uncomfortably long time, he sat staring at her. Finally, he said, "Thanks. For being so great at dinner. You really got my mom off my back."

Her lips pressed into a slight frown, but it quickly smoothed into indifference. "Anytime."

Alone again, Wayne laid back, setting the book aside. He was no longer in the mood to read. His gaze wandered to the closed door. The more time he spent around Val, the more he wished he'd kept his mouth shut and let her leave. Not only did he have to navigate the tumultuous landscape of his family, now he had a pretend relationship with a woman who could barely stand to look at him.

He got up from the stiff mattress and went to the veranda. He looked to the left, where the door to Val's balcony stood open. He tapped a finger on the iron railing, wondering if he could talk her into sharing the bed if he promised to keep his hands to himself.

The lumpy sofa-bed creaked and groaned with every move and was one of the most uncomfortable things he's ever laid on.

A mechanical melody drifted from the open door of Val's room, followed by, "Hey. Did you get my text?" After a brief pause, she said, "Yeah, the drive was intense, but worth it. I know. The mountains are gorgeous." She paused again and added, "I'm sorry for what I said. And you're right. I've been hanging on too hard to the past."

Wayne backed into the living area of the suit, not wanting to eavesdrop on Val's private conversation. He laid down on the uncomfortable mattress, resigning himself to his new sleeping arrangement.

CHAPTER II

VALERIE

VAL WOKE TO THE smell of fresh brewed coffee seeping through the closed bedroom door. Her groggy mind registered the delicious brew, and she dragged herself out of bed to find the source of the wonderful concoction.

She'd spent most of the night trying to lose herself in her book, but she ended up staring at the walls, her mind reeling from the decision she made to stay. What she needed was a long, intense run to flush out the worry twisting inside her gut.

She wandered out of the bedroom, following the delectable aroma. "Oh yes. Sweet nectar of the gods."

Wayne reclined in a chair on the balcony, a carafe on the table beside him. He glanced to the side and nodded to the tray. "Help yourself. I wasn't sure how you took your coffee, so I had them bring everything."

She eyed the dark brew in his cup. "I see you are a simple man."

"I like mine hot and bitter." He took a slow sip. "Just how I prefer my women."

She paused, trying to decide if she was offended or flattered. Ignoring the comment altogether, she poured herself a cup, adding in a generous amount of creamer and sugar. She held the coffee in both hands and leaned over the stone railing. The pale pinks and purples painted the distant sky with their magic, silhouetted the mountains, making them appear to be right out of a fantasy movie.

"What did you have on your itinerary for today?" Wayne asked.

She glanced at the street below. "I planned to spend the day exploring the shops and any other points of interest that catch my eye. Why?"

"We have a brunch date with Sheila, Paul and my parents."

Glancing at her watch, she said, "What time?"

"Around ten."

"Perfect. It gives me time for a quick run."

"Run?"

She nodded across the road. "There's a mountain trail I want to explore. I found it while browsing online. The view from the top is supposed to be amazing."

"Sounds like fun. Mind if I tag along?"

She gave him a curt once over. "You don't have the look of a runner."

"As I'm sure you know from experience, I'm quite athletic."

Turning, she said, "Jogging takes a different kind of stamina."

His eyes cut to the horizon.

"But," she went on. "If you think you can keep up, you're welcome to join me. Wear something light and breathable. I hope you brought comfortable sneakers."

They barely made it out of the lobby and Val took off on a slow jog across the street, anxious to get to the start of the hiking path. The first half mile tilted upward in a slow incline, but once they passed the first overlook, the trail became more winding and difficult. By the time she stopped for her first break, Wayne trudged into view, trying to hide his struggle to breathe.

She took out a bottle of water and her sketch pad, taking a seat on a nearby rock. "We can rest here for a while." She held out the water when he plopped down beside her.

He downed the remaining water in greedy gulps.

"What was that about your stamina?" she asked, keeping her eyes locked on the scenery below.

"Exploring your body is nowhere near as taxing as this trail."

She shot him a sideways frown. "I guess you are used to more amorous lovers."

Instead of answering, he fidgeted with some buttons on his camera.

She opened the sketch book, focusing on the view. A while later, the soft clicking of the camera made her look away from the drawing. Her hand moved without being prompted and began to outline Wayne's shape against the horizon. She rushed to map out his before he moved. She'd worry about the details later. Once his shape was on the paper, she rubbed in shadows, leaving empty space to highlight the reflection of the sun on his profile.

"Impressive."

Val shoved the pencil in the fold of the book and slammed it shut, piercing Wayne with a perturbed glare. Her skin prickled at the fear of him judging her art. "It's okay for an amateur. I'm sure your pictures are way better."

"Good enough to make decent money, I guess."

She tucked her book in the backpack. "I haven't found a way to market my work, so it will stay a hobby for now." Smiling, she added, "Maybe I should branch out into a more lucrative side gig like yourself."

She'd meant the remark to be lighthearted, but when she looked up, he frowned. A second later, he started for the trail. "I think I'm going to head back."

"Hey," She snatched up her backpack and ran after him. "I didn't mean it as an insult."

He whirled on her. "I've come to terms with my choices and what it means for my life. It may not be ideal, but I do what I have to so I'm not beholden to my family and their money."

The frustration in his voice was like a punch in the gut. Aside from the money, she knew all too well the weight of unattainable expectations. Thomas had constantly pressured her to go back to school and pursue something more fulfilling than a mere travel agent. Any time she suggested furthering her love of art, he insinuated she woun't make a real career out of it.

She moved to the side to walk around him, and he held out an arm.

"I didn't mean to snap at you. I just feel like this whole time you've done nothing but judge me when you hardly know anything about my life."

She forced herself to meet his gaze "It's easy for me to sit back and take the moral high ground, given how the world perceives what you do. If I come off as a little intolerant and bitter, it's because I'm still shell-shocked from the whole situation. And yes, I realize it isn't your fault." She readjusted the strap on her shoulder. "How much did Lisa tell you about me? About my past?"

"Not much. She said you were going through something and needed to be reminded there's more to life than work and your apartment."

She went back to the rock and plopped down. "I'm twenty-seven years old. I thought by now I'd be married, have a career, maybe a family. For the last two years I gave my everything to a man I was sure I'd spend the rest of my life with."

"What happened between you two?"

"It's a story as old as time. Girl meets boy. Girl falls head over heels. Then one pregnancy scare later sends the boy on a journey of self-discovery in another woman's vagina. In our bed, no less." The memory made her shudder.

"Afterward, something inside me broke. He shattered my world and ever since then I've been trying to find my way back to the woman I was before. The scariest part of all is the reality that I may never be her again. And I'm so angry he had the power to snuff her out so completely."

Wayne glanced away. When he looked up again, there was a tenderness in his gaze. "Why did you agree to our date?"

Unable to look at him, she said, "Other than being brow beaten into submission by Lisa? I guess I wanted to prove to myself

Thomas wasn't right. That I'm not the problem. That I'm still capable of some kind of meaningful connection with another human being."

"You could have ended things at the restaurant."

Her face flushed. "I know. I wish I had a good answer as to why I went home with a total stranger. Maybe it's because I wanted to feel something other than regret." After another long pause, she pushed out a breathy laugh. "It turns out, even my best friend thinks I'm a lost cause, too. She had to go out of her way to pay some guy to date me."

"Had I known you were clueless about the date—"

She cut him off by standing. "You were doing your job. Which, by the way, you are quite amazing at." She noticed the hint of color framing his face. "Despite what you may think, I'm not angry with you. I'm more upset at myself for letting it get this far. Even after all this time, Thomas still has this creepy hold on me I can't shake off. It's kind of nice, knowing where I stand with you. We have clear expectations and boundaries. I feel like I'm finally in control of my life."

She glanced at her watch. "We should head back if we are going to make our brunch date."

As soon as she started for the path, Wayne hurried in front of her. "I don't know if it matters at this point, but had it been a real date, if we had met in another life, I would have asked you out again."

It did matter. More than she wanted to admit. Of all the men she could have broken her dry spell with, it had to be someone who shared her artistic appreciation and beauty of the world, yet he was as unavailable as any one person can be.

Stepping past him, she said, "Yeah, in another life."

On the hike back down the mountain, she kept her distance both physically and mentally. Her thoughts swirled around their conversation, and even though she believed in the sincerity of what he said, she hoped he was lying. That he told her those things to make her feel better about their tryst.

Just before they reached the road, Wayne jogged to her side and slipped his hand into hers. She stared at the fingers, then glanced up again and realized they were within eyesight of the resort. Of course. He would want to keep up the appearances of a happy couple in front of anyone watching.

She plastered on a silly smile and started swinging her arm back and forth. Wayne hesitated at first, but relaxed and matched her grin as they crossed the street.

To her surprise, when they got into the elevator, he didn't step away from her like he had the night before. Instead, he turned toward her and pulled her into him, his lips hovering over her mouth. The faint hint of coffee lingered on his breath. "Can I kiss you?"

Again, the rational voice inside her head screamed at her, *Tell him no. Move away.* But her head bobbed up and down, betraying her.

She watched from somewhere outside her consciousness, as she clung to his neck. He urged her legs up over his hips and spun her around, pressing her between him and the wall. He pressed into her as if trying to make their bodies share the same space. Their kiss deepened, sending her head spinning from the sheer force of his tongue waging war with her own for dominance.

It wasn't until the bell announced their arrival that he released her, letting her trembling legs ease back to the ground. She tried to say something—anything, but her lips were still on fire from their kiss.

He urged her out of the elevator, squeezing her hand as they made their way to their room. At the door, he said, "You have the key."

She shook herself out of the erotic stupor and fished for the room key in the pack. As soon as the latch clicked, his lips were on her again. He pushed through the door and swung her inside.

His whole body went rigid, then took a step away from her. Val looked over her shoulder to the stranger sitting on the couch, staring at them.

"What the hell are you doing here?" Wayne asked.

The woman stood, her lips spreading into a ravenous smile. "Is that any way to greet your girlfriend?"

CHAPTER 12

WAYNE

"Ex-girlfriend," Wayne said, stepping around Val. "How did you get in here?"

Rita raised an eyebrow as she stared at the obvious erection pushing at the fabric of his shorts. "Jennifer was nice enough to let me in." She glanced at Val. "Who is this lovely woman?"

Wayne looked at Valerie, almost forgetting she was in the same room. "This is my friend—my date for the wedding." He pushed out a long breath. "Valerie."

Rita's smile didn't falter. "It's lovely to meet you, Valerie. Would you be a dear and give Wayne and I some time alone? We have a lot to catch up on."

Val cut her eyes to him, and when he didn't answer right away, something shifted in her demeanor. To Rita, he said, "That's not going to happen. You need to leave."

Unfazed by his dismissal, Rita stood. "Jennifer mentioned you brought a date, but from the way she described your interactions, I didn't think you two were so—" She motioned to the both of them. "Passionate for each other. I supposed I may have been a little forward to assume we could have the chance to hash out our tarnished past, but you deserve an explanation."

Wayne glanced at Val again, her expression a dangerous mixture of shock and anger. He couldn't blame her. He, too, was furious with his mom for having the audacity to assume anything about him and Val. Sure, their relationship was fake, but no one else knew about their arrangement.

He went to the door and pulled it open. "Please go. Don't ever come into my room unannounced again." Even as he spoke, he regretted his choice of words.

Rita came to a stop in front of him, her usual unbothered bravado slipping. "If you would have taken my calls—"

He gaped at her, a surged of renewed betrayal fueled his resentment. "You made it clear how you felt when you disappeared from my life. I moved on. I thought you did too."

Rita's eyes darted to the side where Val stood watching them. "I'm staying in the suite next to your parents. I'd like to give you my side of things."

A tiny part of him was morbidly curious to find out the truth. He wanted closure. The bedroom door slammed shut, making him wince. He motioned to the hallway. "It doesn't matter why."

Rita left without another word, and he fought the urge to slam the door just as Val had done when she disappeared into the bedroom. He crossed the living room, resting a hand on the knob and tapping his knuckles lightly on the door. "Can I come in?"

"No." Her tone was tight.

"Can we talk about this? I didn't know Rita was going to just waltz into my suite."

The door opened so quickly, he had to step back or fall over the threshold.

"Our suite," she snapped. "And there's really nothing to talk about, friend."

She went to close the door again, but he put a hand up to hold it open. "That's not fair. I was flustered, and in shock."

Her lips thinned into a grim smile. "You don't have to explain. If you want to go after her, be my guest." She dropped her eyes to the floor and walked to the bed, where she grabbed the clothes she'd laid out. "Just make up your mind about where we go from here before I get anymore entangled in your...family drama."

She closed herself in the bathroom. A few seconds later, he heard the shower turn on. For a long time, he stood in the doorway, considering what Val said. Did he really want closure from Rita? He'd spent the last year and a half coming to terms with how easily he was manipulated and lied to by a woman he thought he would marry, spend the rest of his life with. The same heart he walled up night after night with random women for meaningless sex. A heart he feared would never heal enough to trust anyone again.

He backed away from the door, anger rising inside his chest. It wasn't Rita he wanted to confront. The audacity of his mother to continue to push her agenda after repeatedly telling her to back off. If he hadn't been there for the sole reason to support his sister, he would have packed up and left, but he refused to ruin this for Shiela.

He changed into the clothes he'd set out before leaving for the run, intending to confront his mom about Rita's presence and demand she make his ex leave. He had just stepped into the hallway when Shiela walked by. She saw the frown on his face and slowed to a stop beside him.

"Why the sour look? Uh oh, trouble in paradise?"

Wayne smoothed the frown into a slightly less angry grimace. "She's gone too far."

"Who? Valerie?"

"No. My mother. She gave Rita a key to my room."

His sister's mouth dropped open. "What is wrong with that woman? Did something happen between Rita and Val?"

"Not exactly. When we got back to the room this morning, she was waiting for me."

Sheila crossed her arms, giving him one of her famous unreadable once overs. "Go on."

"As soon as I got over the shock, I made Rita leave. Now, Val refuses to talk to me."

"Of course she's upset. Your ex-girlfriend just sauntered into your room out of nowhere." His inability to look his sister in the eye made her drop her arms to her side. "What exactly did you say?"

"I might have gotten a bit flustered and called Val a friend."

Sheila's eyes widened, and she raised her hands, balling them into fists. "I can't believe you would say something so stupid. It's no wonder Val is so upset." Sheila's tone took on a sharpness he wasn't used to. "I know you, Wayne. Why you push people away. But if you want any kind of future with Val, you're going to have to stop treating your relationship like a transaction and start acting like she matters."

Her words cut through his anger, leaving him feeling exposed. "It's not like that. We—" He stopped himself before confessing their relationship really was transactional. His gaze slid to the window at the end of the hall. He didn't know why Val was so upset about being called a friend when, in reality, they were barely acquaintances. To Val, he was simply a means to an end. A necessary inconvenience for her to enjoy the vacation.

"Where is Val now?"

"In the shower."

"Go downstairs with Daddy and Paul. I'm going to do you a favor and try to save your relationship."

He started to argue, but that would lead to certain truths coming to light. "Alright, but don't push her to open up if she doesn't want to." He regretted the words as soon as they rolled off his tongue. Sheila didn't react, so she probably didn't catch on to his paranoia. All he could do now was the chance to dislodge his foot from his mouth. First, he would confront his mother.

CHAPTER 13

VALERIE

VAL'S SKIN GLOWED BRIGHT red by the time she stepped out of the shower. The near scalding water did a good job of burning away most of her anger, but a dangerous fury simmered just beneath the surface. She refused to let go of it, lest she was forced to confront the jealousy lingering inside her chest. No matter how vehemently she told herself she had nothing to be jealous about, her mind conjured the longing on Wayne's stupid face. He may have been surprised to see Rita, but he wasn't as disappointed as he claimed.

In the bedroom, she stormed to the closet and picked out a loose-fitting gray t-shirt along with a pair of dark denim jeans. Before Rita showed up, she planned to wear a pale blue sundress, wanting to make a good impression on his family. Now, she couldn't care less what they thought of her. It was painfully obvious Jennifer preferred Rita to Val.

She stood at the end of the bed, staring at the closet where her luggage waited. Her fingers opened and closed as she contemplated leaving. It would be so easy to pack up her things and go back to New Mexico. Not even a free vacation was worth the drama lurking around every corner of this family. Wayne could deal with the fallout of their lies. He deserved a helping of humility after everything he'd done.

Someone knocked on the bedroom door, sending her pulse to racing. "I'll be out in a minute." She snapped.

After a brief pause, Sheila's voice broke through the silence. "Wayne said you were running behind. I thought we could walk down together."

Val slumped forward, fighting a groan. The last thing she wanted to do was be rude to Shiela. Not when she had been nothing but kind and welcoming. Plastering a fake smile on her face, she opened the door. "Sorry about that. I thought you were someone else.

If Shiela was offended, she didn't show it. "I don't know about you, but I'm starving. This place has the best strawberries and cream crepes in the northern hemisphere."

Val eyed the beige blouse Sheila wore. It looked freshly pressed and coordinated perfectly with her taupe pants. "Would you mind giving me a few minutes? I need to finish dressing."

Shiela smiled. "Okay, but hurry. I want to get something to eat before the guy's scarf everything down."

Alone again, Val snatched up the sundress and quickly changed. She joined Shiela in the living room. "I'm ready. Let's go."

At the elevators, Shiela pushed the call button, then turned to Val and said, "Wayne told me what happened with Rita."

Val kept her gaze on the reflective doors. "Did he?"

"And he admitted to being a complete and utter moron by referring to you as a friend."

Val wasn't sure how she should feel about Wayne being so upfront and open with Sheila. He claimed no one in his family knew about his extra income. "That's an understatement," she muttered. "I know, it's a stupid thing to be mad about." Val glanced at the woman beside her. "I overreacted."

"He's lucky you didn't take more drastic measures." The bell dinged, and she stepped inside. When Val joined her, she hit the button that would take them to the lobby. "Wayne isn't exactly known for his keen sense of foresight. He didn't mean to insult you or belittle your relationship."

Val stared at the numbers above the double doors, willing them to hurry. "I think the shock of seeing Rita in our room made me lose touch with reality for a few seconds."

Shiela let out a soft laugh. "She has that effect on people. And always in a bad way. I'll make sure it doesn't happen again."

All Val wanted to do was confess their ruse, but she kept her eyes averted to the ground. "I take it you don't care for her."

"Hell no. Jennifer set them up because Rita is the daughter of some douchey attorney friend." Sheila bent forward to catch Val's attention. "You have nothing to worry about. I can promise you, Wayne is not interested in reliving that terrible part of his past."

Sheila didn't see his face earlier. A look of desire for something so tangible, yet so out of reach. Now, for Wayne he had the chance to reclaim something dear to him that had been lost. There had been a time Val would have given anything for the same opportunity.

None of it mattered, though. If Wayne decided to pursue his ex, he was technically a single man. Val was simply a temporary placeholder in his life. She had no claim to him, nor did she want one. But it didn't make the situation any less hurtful. For the purpose of the wedding, she and Wayne were supposed to be a couple. For this one week, he was meant to be hers. Maybe Thomas was right, after all. Maybe Val was the problem.

CHAPTER 14

WAYNE

B‍Y THE TIME HE made it to the lobby, Wayne was still trying to piece together the truth of Val's reaction. What if the roles had been reversed, and Val casually dismissed him to the friend zone for an ex? It didn't matter about their agreement. To the rest of the world and to his family, Valerie was his girlfriend. He didn't think he would have reacted so strongly, given the reality of their situation, but there were certain expectations and appearances they needed to adhere to.

A voice in the back of his mind tried to hint at the possibility of Val being more emotionally invested in their ruse than she let on, but he quickly banished the thought. No woman of her caliber could overlook his past and disregard his questionable life choices for the chance to pursue something meaningful.

The sound of his mother's laughter reignited his anger, and he stormed through the doors to the outer patio. His dad and Paul were already sitting at the table, their backs to him. His mother stood next to the entryway, talking to someone he recognized but couldn't recall a name.

As soon as she saw him, her smile faltered, but didn't fall away completely. "Wayne, is something the matter?"

He eyed the other woman, who took one look at his scowl and excused herself. When they were alone, he said, "What the hell is wrong with you?"

Jennifer leaned back, her brilliant green eyes narrowing. "You better have a good reason for using such a tone with me."

"How could you give Rita a key to my room?"

"I did no such thing."

"She said you let her in."

"I simply had the maid unlock the door for her. I thought it would be a pleasant surprise."

"How many times do I have to tell you to stay out of my personal life? Rita and I are over. I can't believe you want us to get back together after what she did."

Jennifer dismissed his comment with a wave of her meticulously manicured hand. "It was a mistake. She realizes that now."

He took a step back and raised a finger at her. "I expect you to apologize to Valerie."

"Apologize for what? She's not right for you or our family. You and Rita—"

Wayne leaned into her, lowering his voice. "This is my life. You don't have a say in it."

Jennifer's mouth clamped shut, her eyes betraying the shock of his outburst.

"Rita is in my past. I am here with Valerie. Am I clear?"

After a minute of staring at each other, she smoothed a nonexistent wrinkle from her blouse. "Extremely."

He didn't give her a chance to say anything else before joining the others at the table. His anger melted into relief when he saw Val taking a seat next to his dad.

Sheila dropped into the chair beside Paul. "Sorry we're late."

He kissed her cheek. "If it wasn't for your lack of time awareness, we wouldn't have met, so please never change."

She gave his arm a halfhearted swat.

Val glanced around the table, and when she spotted Wayne approaching, the tender smile she wore vanished. Her gaze slid away from him to the surrounding scenery.

Wayne's dad leaned closer to her and said, "I saw you and Wayne heading to the trails this morning."

"I wanted to go for a jog." A whisper of the smile returned. "The view is breathtaking."

Sheila laughed. "Wayne jogged? Voluntarily?"

"Is that so hard to believe?" Wayne made sure whatever anger still lingered inside him didn't show in his words or his face. He sat down on the other side of Val, ignoring the way she inched to the side.

The forced smile on her face tilted into something more mischievous. "He barely survived."

Her comment drew a round of laughter from the table.

Sheila turned to Wayne. "I can't believe you got him to agree to go outdoors." She reached across the table and pinched at his cheek. "I think he's afraid too much sunlight might wilt his handsome face."

Wayne ducked away, fighting off the embarrassed traces of heat extending up his neck and into his face. He reached for Val's hand, but she slipped it out of his grasp with the pretense of grabbing the mimosa in front of her.

"I talked to Leon this morning," Paul said. "He's disappointed that he's been bumped from the wedding party, but he's still coming for the ceremony."

Wayne sat forward, remembering the accident. "I heard about the wreck. How's Abigale?"

"She's out of the hospital and home." Sheila said. "Jeremy says she's recovering well. Only a few scrapes and bruises." She tapped a finger on the table, chewing at her lower lip. Wayne could practically hear the wheels turning in her head, making him nervous about the thought process going on up there.

She looked at Paul. "I know how much you want Leon to be in the wedding. What if there is a way he can still keep his role as a groomsman?"

Sheila then smiled at Val. "Abigale is about your size. I realize this is last minute, but would you consider being a bridesmaid? Her dress is in my room, and we still have time to make any alterations. I'm sure Wayne would love for you to be part of the ceremony as well." She eyed Wayne, the subtle shift in her mouth insisting he agree.

The thought of sharing such an intimate moment with Val both excited and scared him. "I think that's a great idea," he said.

Val stared at them, confused. "I thought Rita was taking her place. Jennifer mentioned it when I—we arrived."

Sheila's smile soured. "Is that why she's here?" Turning to their dad, she said, "You need to control your wife."

"I didn't know anything about it."

Turning back to Val, Sheila composed herself again. "I will not have that woman standing by my side on my wedding day."

Wayne half expected Val to bolt from the table by the way her body was poised at the edge of her seat. After a few seconds, she relaxed into the chair. "Are you sure? You don't even know me."

"We have the next couple of days to remedy that."

Val glanced to the side, probably to gauge Wayne's reaction. Despite their earlier confrontation, the smile splitting his lips was genuine, and he gave her a slight nod. Turning back to Shiela, she said, "Sure. I mean, of course. I'd be honored."

"Fantastic." Sheila grabbed Paul's arm. "Tell Leon he's still in the wedding."

Wayne leaned over. "Thank you for doing this."

Val kept her eyes locked on the mimosa and shrugged. "What are friends for?"

Her comment cut deep, but he didn't have the chance to dwell on the veiled meaning when his phone vibrated in his pants. He immediately recognized the name, and, not wanting to get into a conversation with a client in front of his family, he excused himself from the table.

"Where are you going?" His dad asked. "We haven't eaten yet."

"Work stuff." He made it inside the lobby and glanced over his shoulder. Val stared at him, her mouth set in a slight frown.

Her attention drifted to Shiela, and he tamped down the twinge of guilt fluttering inside his stomach. He shot a quick text to the missed call, explaining he was out of town, and shoved the phone back into his pants.

Instead of joining the others again, he stood to the side of the open doorway, watching Val. He wanted to ask her to talk in private, but he didn't know what he would say to her. She made him feel things he hadn't experienced in a long time. Would he ever be ready to confront those feelings again?

A woman approach him. Rita stepped in front of him, blocking his view, "I wish you would let me explain myself. I owe you that much. If you never want to talk or see me again afterward, at least you will know the truth."

Wayne knew her too well to believe she would give up so easily. Rita's unwavering tenacity and ambition were some of the things he'd both loved and hated about her. But if a simple talk would get her off his back and out of his life again, he would take the chance.

"Alright." He motioned to a table. "We can talk."

CHAPTER 15

VALERIE

Val pretended Wayne's abrupt departure wasn't weighing on her conscience. Didn't he have the decency to put his little side job on hold for a few days? He was there to celebrate his sister's wedding, after all. But it wasn't her place to tell him how to run his business or his life.

"Valerie."

Val looked up from the barely touched food on her plate. Sheila's piercing stare unnerved her.

"Is everything okay?"

"Of course. Just lost in thought." No longer hungry, Val pushed away from the table. "I think I'm going to explore for a little while."

"Would you like some company?"

"No, stay. Enjoy your meal. If Wayne comes back, tell him I'll catch up with him later." She didn't expect him to return. He was going to have quite a few calls to deal with while away.

She wanted to go upstairs and grab her purse, but the thought of catching him on the phone with a client was less than appealing, so she decided window shopping would have to keep her busy until she was ready to face Wayne again. The second she stepped foot inside the arched door, she spotted him sitting at a table near the far corner of the bar area. And he wasn't alone.

His back was to her, but Rita had the perfect view of what must have been a dire look of shock that came over Val's face. The subtle shift in the other woman's demeanor caught Val's attention. Nothing overt, but enough for her to notice a softening of her mouth and one side of her lips lifted into a hint of a smirk.

Val had an overwhelming urge to go over to their table and make a scene. She tried to convince herself it wasn't jealousy making her react that way. It was the idea of competition and control. Val had lost Thomas to another woman, and here she was about to lose another, even if Wayne wasn't hers to claim. Rita didn't know their dynamic and played the game to steal back someone she thought was already taken.

A fit of laughter threatened to bubble up from somewhere deep inside the unstable cascade of emotions writhing around her heart. She clamped her mouth shut to keep from bursting out into hysterics. It occurred to her that she had fantasized about this exact moment with Thomas, but she was the one sitting in Rita's place.

Movement across from Rita brought Val back from her epiphany. His expression, though guarded, betrayed his guilt. Val relaxed her face and body, giving both of them a slight smile before continuing on her way to the lobby. Behind her, Wayne called her name, but she ignored him until he caught up to her outside.

She spun around when he started to speak, cutting him off. "Jesus Christ, Wayne. I told you already, I have my own plans. Stop following me like some lost puppy. I just want some time to myself." The vehemence of her words shocked even her.

He stared at her for a few seconds, his face pinching in confusion, then it relaxed into indifference. "I'm sorry I bothered you. I'll leave you alone."

Her legs started to carry her after him, but she stopped herself. It didn't matter if he was angry, or if she hurt his feelings. Theirs was a simple contract between two consenting adults. But the turmoil swirling inside her chest wasn't so cut and dry. When he passed by the elevators, she thought it assumed safe to go to their room.

Once she was outside again, she went to the edge of the concrete sidewalk, staring across the street, waiting for the little green man to tell her to cross. By the time she made it to the other side, she questioned her decision to agree to be in the wedding. If she told Sheila she wanted to back out, inevitably, the truth would come out that she and Wayne had been lying to them. But really, what did it matter? It wasn't like she was ever going to see them again.

For the next half hour, she wandered through the main square, where she stopped at a few places to window shop from outside. She came across a little antique store and went inside. Maybe she could find something for Lisa to help mend their friendship. Their shared love of vintage decor had brought them together in the first place.

Val took her time meandering through the tight spaces filled with antique furniture and wall decor. It didn't take her long to find a well-used and tarnished pewter brush set that came with a small hand mirror. The glass was in pristine condition, given how aged the base looked. Even if the mirror wasn't the original, Lisa would go crazy over them.

Val glanced at the price and cringed. She was about to set them back down when a thought occurred to her. She wasn't paying for her room, which left her with a significant budget to play with. And Lisa was worth every penny. They had been there for each other in the best and worst of times. Val truly believed Lisa had her best interest at heart when she hired Wayne. In fact, the date was exactly what she needed to put her past behind her. Whatever longing she may have felt for Thomas had turned to disgust.

On her way to the cash register, she spotted an old Kodak Brownie camera sitting on a glass table display, surrounded by other photography accessories. The first person she thought about when she saw the camera was Wayne. The price tag lay face up on the tray. She didn't have a lot of knowledge about those types of cameras, but the thirty-dollar price was something she couldn't pass up. Not when it looked to be in such good condition, and from what she could see of the case, all the accessories seemed to be intact.

As soon as she had the camera in hand, she paused, staring at the aged leather case, wondering what Wayne would think of her giving him something like that. It was a simple gift and didn't cost a lot of money. Surely, he'd know the value. Squeezing tighter to the camera, she gave herself a quick nod. First, she would apologize for snapping at him. She didn't have the right to tell him who he could be around, and if it looked bad to the rest of the family, well, that was his problem.

After making her purchase, she continued her exploration, heading for the open field near the edge of town where a tall gate read: Circle K Ranch. A group of people were perched around a wooden corral where a man dressed the part of a ranch hand, worked with a beautiful palomino in the center ring.

Not being a big fan of horses, she kept her distance and wandered around to the side where she saw an open barn with other farm animals she might be able to pet. She made it halfway to the barn when someone spoke behind her.

"Are you lost?"

Val jumped and spun around, coming face to snout with a gray and white dapple horse. The man sitting in the saddle smiled down at her. A pair of shaded eyes caught her in their vibrant, light gray depths.

The man nodded toward the pen. "You should probably stay with your group."

Following his stare, she said, "Oh, I'm not with them." She motioned behind her. "I'm staying at the resort."

His smile widened, and he hopped out of the saddle, landing beside her with the ease of a man who'd spent his whole life on horseback. "Are you here for the wedding?"

She hesitated. "Yeah."

"You here for the bride or the groom?"

"The bride," she said, cautious about his sudden interest, thinking she should have said no. "Why? Do you know her family?"

"I know their money. I used to ride with their kids when we were younger. It's Sheila's wedding, isn't it?"

Val nodded.

"I had used to have the biggest crush on her." His eyes slid down her body in a calculating manner. "I don't think I've ever seen you before. Are you a friend of the family?"

She wasn't sure which category she fit into, but she certainly couldn't tell him the truth. "I suppose you could say that. I'm here with her brother."

He stood up straighter. "I see. So, you're Wayne's girlfriend?"

"Not exactly." She reached out and stroked the horse's mane in an attempt to subdue the nervous ball forming in her stomach. His close proximity and easy smile made her pulse race in ways that left her confused about her feelings for Wayne.

He watched her movements. "Just friends, then?"

"You could say that."

His lips widened into what she could best describe as a satisfied grin. He held out a hand. "I'm Eric."

Taking it, she said, "Valerie—Val." When he brought it to his mouth, she had the overwhelming urge to snatch it away, but managed to keep still. His lips were soft against her skin.

"Well, Val, are you in a hurry to get back to the resort?"

"Not really."

"Great. How about I take you on an exclusive tour? The valley is beautiful this time of year."

"I don't know. Horses make me uncomfortable. I had a bad experience when I was a kid."

He took the reins of his horse and nodded to the barn on the other side of the corral. "Then why don't I get you more acquainted with Bastian. He's good with timid riders."

The idea of a distraction from Wayne and the wedding was too good to pass up. "Lead the way."

CHAPTER 16

WAYNE

WAYNE STOOD ON THE balcony, phone in hand. He had typed out a text to Sheila, making an excuse for Val to have to leave. The venom in her words sparked an irrational anger. So much so, it made him rethink the decision to have her be a part of the wedding. He wasn't even sure he wanted her to stay in the same room as him anymore. Not since Rita had he felt so humiliated. But he had done the same thing to her. But Val didn't know he only talked to Rita to get some closure, then he wouldn't speak to her ever again.

The screen on his phone went black without him sending the message. He trudged back inside and, against his better judgment, pulled out Val's luggage to pack her belongings. He'd call another hotel and book her a room for the rest of her vacation. It was the least he could do since it had been his dumb suggestion that got her in this situation.

He reached for the sketchbook on the nightstand, intending to tuck it between some clothes, when he noticed a familiar face on the bookmarked page. The detail shading of his features against the black and white mountain scape was incredible. Her lines captured a man he hadn't seen in years. For the first time, he saw how she perceived him. She looked beyond the walls he carefully constructed and peered into his very soul.

Curiosity outweighed any reservations he had about invading her privacy, and he flipped through the book, marveling at the raw beauty of each imperfect rendition. Such imperfections made her drawings spectacular; more so than his most posed and processed photographs.

He let his arm drop, and looked around the room, his eyes landing on the open suitcase, its bright pink color a symbol of the vibrant, beautiful woman it belonged to. She was a stark contrast to his measured world. The brief but vulnerable moment they shared on the mountain awakened a longing inside him. It had been a whisper of something he didn't realize he'd been missing until now. Maybe it's why he so eagerly tried to get away from her. The thought of leaving himself vulnerable again made his chest tighten, making it hard to breathe.

Embarrassed, he put everything back the way he found it, not wanting Val to know he had seen her private drawings. Instead of returning to the balcony, he headed for the elevators, hoping to catch up with her. He wasn't sure what he would say, but they needed to talk about what happened between them in the elevator.

As soon as the doors opened on the ground floor, he saw his dad making his way through the lobby alone. It didn't surprise Wayne. His parents were avoiding each other. He never understood how they were happy, living like they did. What kind of fulfillment could a loveless marriage give two people?

It was one of the many reasons he didn't visit his family more often, nor did he want to end up like them. After Rita disappeared from his life, he now realized that she'd done him a favor. Had they stayed together, their relationship would have eventually turned distant and miserable. Just like his parents.

Yet there was a familiar comfort he missed with Rita. His loneliness was magnified on those nights between clients. When he saw her in the room earlier, the spark, however small and brief, had ignited a pathetic sadness inside him. Not for the lost relationship, but for what it represented.

He fully understood, then, just how horrible it must have been to watch a ghost from his past appear out of nowhere. Would he have been any less angry had their roles been reversed?

"Going for a walk?"

Wayne glanced over his shoulder where his dad snagged a newspaper from the table near the fountain. "Yeah. I saw Val heading into town and thought I'd join her."

"Maybe you can take her to that little bistro downtown. Give you two a chance to spend some time away from all this chaos."

The thought of spending some time alone with Val caused his stomach to roll into a nervous ball. "Did she say anything after I left?"

"Just that she would catch up with you later." He settled into a high-back chair near the floor-to-ceiling windows with a magnificent view of the mountains.

Outside, Wayne headed in the same direction Val had gone, hoping to spot her in one a window of a shop along the main strip. He made it to the edge of the stables without seeing any sign of her. Turning to the crowd milling around the range, he didn't see her there, either. A familiar face stepped out of the barn, carrying a saddle.

He wandered up the gravel road leading up to the office. "Mr. Walsh."

The years of ranching had weathered the old man's face, yet he didn't look much different from the last time Wayne saw him nearly eight years ago. "There's a face I'd recognize anywhere," Joseph boomed, taking Wayne's hand in his calloused palm.

"It's good to see you, sir." Wayne glanced around the corrals. "Looks like this place has really done well over the years."

Joseph followed Wayne's stare and nodded. "Eric's been the one to do most of the upkeep. He's got a gift with people and horses. Unlike myself. I'd rather talk shop with a palomino than a tourist."

"How is Eric? I haven't talked to him since we went off to college."

"He got his master's in finance, and I thought he would move away, start his own business. But the ranch is in his blood. He moved back a few years ago to help me out." Mr. Walsh leaned in, giving Wayne a conspiratorial smile. "Don't tell Eric, but he has really brought life back into this place. If it wasn't for him, I would have shut the ranch down already.

Despite how their friendship ended, Wayne was glad to hear Eric did so well for himself. "Is he around? I'd like to catch up." Maybe apologize for being such a snobby asshole.

Mr. Walsh craned his neck, glancing around the open space. "I saw him talking to one of the guests earlier. I think he wanted to take her on a tour of the valley, but I saw them earlier near the small corral."

Wayne's mouth parted into a wide grin. "Always the lady's man."

"And a gentleman." Joseph added. "Anyway, I need to get back to it."

Wayne wandered through the familiar landscape of the ranch, marveling at how little everything changed over the years. He had a lot of wonderful memories at there. But that was before he and Eric let their rivalries go too far. Eric had always been the golden boy—easygoing and charming, the type who could laugh off failure and shrug off success.

Their rivalry started small, then it quickly grew into something more intense when they tried to one up each other in every aspect of their lives. Even the girls they dated. Everything came to a head when Eric began dating a girl he knew Wayne had a crush on. There was no taking back those angry words shouted at one another. It was a rift neither man could over come. Wayne and Eric didn't speak again after that summer, and Wayne regretted letting his pride ruin a good friendship.

He rounded the corner of the barn and halted when he saw the two people in the fenced corral. Eric stood next to a dapple mare. Val kept her distance, her body tense and withdrawn from the horse, yet she wore a pleased smile on her face. She tentatively reached out a hand and stroked the mare's silky mane. She gave it a few strokes, then took a step back.

Wayne tried to tamp down the surge of jealousy heating his blood. He told himself it was the remnants of the deeply rooted rivalry between him and Eric, and not the idea that Val was showing interest in another man. They weren't really dating, after all. Just like he was free to pursue another woman, even Rita, if he was so inclined, Val too could do the same.

But why did it have to be Eric?

Pushing off the sun heated wood, Wayne headed back to the resort, unsure of where to go from there.

CHAPTER 17

VALERIE

VAL STILL SMILED WHEN she returned. Despite her aversion to horses, Eric had made her feel at ease around them. His pleasant demeanor and somewhat cheesy flirting helped distract her from everything else going on. When he asked her out to dinner, she was quick to turn him down. She wasn't interested in adding more complications to an already difficult situation.

She waited for an elevator to come down when she spotted Wayne heading into the bar. Glancing down at the bag in her hand, she considered taking the camera up to their room and sitting it out on the table for him to find. But after how she'd spoken to him earlier, she wanted to apologize and give him the peace offering.

Wayne sat on a stool at the end of the bar, slumped forward, a glass of dark beer in front of him. She hopped onto the seat next to him and waved at the bartender. "I'll have what he's having."

Wayne looked to the side, but didn't meet her stare. Okay, he was still mad, apparently. The bartender slid a glass to her. She took a long sip, working up the courage to down the crow she was about to eat when he leaned back and met her stare.

"Did you enjoy your little adventure?"

The bite of his words made her gut clench. Was he still angry with her? "What is that supposed to mean?"

Returning to his beer, he said, "Nothing."

She took in a long, steadying breath. "Look, about what I said earlier—"

He cut her off by standing and reaching into his back pocket, pulling out his wallet. "It doesn't matter. I'm probably going to hang out with my dad and watch the game with him, so you will have the rest of the evening to yourself."

She stared at him, unsure of what to say. Her eyes went to the bag in her hand, but before she could reach for the camera, he slipped by her.

At the entrance of the bar, he paused. "Maybe you can visit the ranch again. Go for a tour. The valley is beautiful at twilight."

After a few seconds, understanding swept over her. "Were you spying on me?"

He swung an incredulous look at her. "Of course not. I happen to be visiting an old friend when I saw you and Eric together."

She recognized the sharp tone of jealousy, and it made her even more confused. "So what? I'm not allowed to find my own entertainment?"

"How do you think it looks if my girlfriend is throwing herself at some ranch hand when she's supposed to be here with me?"

Her mouth dropped open, and the only thing she could think to say was, "Yeah, because that's so much worse than watching my boyfriend turn into a pining, babbling idiot when his ex-shows up out of nowhere."

He ran his fingers through his hair, his mouth twisting further into a frustrated frown. "That's not what happened, and you know it."

Val crossed her arms. "Is that so? I suppose she surprised you at brunch too?"

His jaw flexed back and forth, and she could practically hear the gears turning in his mind. He relaxed his face and backed up a step. "This was a mistake."

"Well, you're the one that has a problem with me enjoying my vacation."

"I'm referring to asking you to stay. I'm going to see if I can find another room for the rest of the week. Or bunk with someone else."

She stared at his back until he disappeared into the lobby. For a long time, she watched the open doorway, trying to wrap her head around what had just happened. After a while, she turned, avoiding eye contact with the bartender, who pretended to clean the counter across from the bar top.

Someone took the seat to her right. Greg nodded to the man behind the bar. "Afternoon, Jene. Can I have a whiskey?" Once he had his drink, he turned his attention to Val. "I ran into Wayne just now. I hope I'm not overstepping, but I recognize the remnants of a lover's quarrel, having been in my fair share."

Val twirled the coaster in front of her. "It's nothing. Just a stupid misunderstanding." One she was still trying to process.

"I'm sure I don't have to tell you how stubborn Wayne can be. It's a trait he inherited from his mother. But it makes them the unstoppable forces of nature they are." He took his time, swirling the amber liquid before downing the contents in one gulp, grimacing slightly. "I tried to instill some of my patience in him. I catch a glimpse of it sometimes."

"Well, he's not the overbearing harpy Jennifer is, so yeah, I'd say you did an okay job." As soon as the words left her mouth, she regretted them. "That was uncalled for. I'm sorry."

Greg didn't try to hide his amusement. "No, you are spot on." He twirled the glass around with one hand. "Sometimes I wish I made different choices. After Sheila's mother died, I was desperate to find someone to fill a maternal role."

When he met Val's gaze, she saw an endearment she missed from her father. "I've caught Wayne looking at you the same way I did Shiela's mother. I wonder what my life would have been like if she lived."

"If you don't mind me asking, what made you choose Jennifer?"

He considered her question for a few seconds. "Duty to the family. Pressure from my parents. There are certain expectations we McNabs must uphold." His smile held genuine joy. "I'm so thankful Sheila found Paul. He makes her happy. That's what I want for both of my children."

"I think Wayne still has feelings for Rita," Val blurted. She felt like she would burst if she didn't get the words out.

Greg captured her stare with the same intensity as his son. "You didn't witness the devastation that woman left in her wake when she disappeared. He loved her at one time, sure, but the broken man she left behind would never take her back."

"Yeah, well, you didn't see the way he acted when she showed up in our room. And earlier—I recognize the look of unresolved feelings when I see them."

"Unresolved doesn't mean those feelings are good."

She stared into the dark amber depths of her drink. "But it complicates things for us."

"I can talk to him."

She shook her head. "This isn't your problem. I shouldn't have said anything." She went to pay for her drink, and Greg pushed her money back at her.

"I've got this."

Back in the lobby, she considered her next move. Really, the only option she had was to pack her bags and head home. She hated the idea of disappointing Sheila. Of everyone Val met so far, she had been the nicest to her. Maybe Wayne should be the one to break the news. He owed Val that much.

CHAPTER 18

WAYNE

Wayne sat at the table, staring into the cloudless sky. Shame mixed with indignant anger. He wanted to bite off his own tongue for what he said to Val. The raw jealousy over catching her with Eric wasn't a simple throwback to a stupid rivalry. It wouldn't have mattered what man had been there with her. He would still feel the same.

The door to the suit open and closed. He turned his head to the side, following Val until she disappeared into the bedroom. He wouldn't let it end like this. Even if he couldn't admit the growing feelings between them, he wasn't going to let her believe she was the problem.

At the door, he paused with his hand braced to turn the knob. He didn't bother knocking, relieved when the door pushed open. Val crossed the room on her way back from the closet, carrying her suitcase to the bed. She flipped it open and went to the chest of drawers and grabbed a handful of clothes, spearing him with a glare on the way by.

She shoved the clothes into the suitcase, not bothering to fold them. It was yet another quirk about her he found unbelievably endearing. Her chaos clashed with his pristine world, and he didn't want to imagine his life when that spark of color faded from it. He took a step into the room. "What are you doing?"

"What does it look like? Leaving. Isn't that what you want?"

He tried to block her path to the closet. "Of course not. I shouldn't have said it."

She stepped around him, giving herself a wide berth. "This was definitely a mistake. I should have just gone back home when I found out about the mixup with my room."

He played with the idea of taking her by the arms. Making her listen to him as he confessed just how much she changed his life in the short time they've known each other. When he was in her presence, his world didn't seem so small and suffocating.

Instead, he stayed just inside the doorway, searching for some other reason to make her change her mind. "What about Sheila? You promised to be in her wedding. You can hate me all you want, but please don't take it out on her."

She stared at him for a long time and no matter how hard he tried, he couldn't make out the truth behind those beautiful eyes.

Seizing on the hesitation, he added, "I'll stay out of the suite when you're here. You won't have to see me until the wedding. I'll even cover for you if you want to spend more time with Eric."

Her shoulders fell, and she sat down on the side of the bed. "It wasn't like that. I just needed to get out of my own head for a while, you know? Eric was simply a distraction." She stood again, returning to packing. "This whole thing we have together is turning into more than I bargained for." She turned her head to the side, eyes locked on the ground. "I'm supposed to be on vacation. I should be enjoying myself, and I'm not. If I wanted this kind of drama, I'd go back to Texas."

Before he could respond, someone knocked on the door. His stomach dropped at the thought of it being Rita, or worse, his mom. He saw the same dread edging its way onto Val's face. He rushed to the door. His muscles relaxed at the sight of Shiela's chipper grin.

She held up a white garment bag. "I brought the bridesmaid dress so Val can try it on. See if it needs adjusting." She swept past him and went to stand by Val, who waited just inside the doorway to the bedroom. "Honestly, I don't think we will have to do anything drastic."

Val stared at the dress, refusing to touch it.

"It won't bite," Sheila said, before shoving the bag into Val's arms.

A demure smile lit up Val's face when Sheila unzipped the bag. "Wow. I've ever seen such a gorgeous dress."

"The back is tricky, but worth the effort. You'll see when you put it on."

Wayne shuffled across the living room and stared at the bedroom door. Frustration made him run his fingers through his hair. Maybe he was deluding himself. No matter what he felt, Val wasn't interested in him the same way.

The door opened, and he swallowed back a groan. The pale-yellow dress wrapped around Val's body as if it had been custom made to fit her every curve.

"Well?" Shiela said, spinning Val around to show off the delicate lattice work at her back. "What do you think?"

His pulse quickened when Val used her hands to smooth down the fabric in the front. He wanted so badly to run his hands palms over her waist and undo the clasps on the back, letting the gown fall to the floor so he could enjoy her naked body again.

Shiela stepped in front of Val to adjust the bodice, and the spell was broken. He cleared his throat. "It's beautiful."

Val glanced up. A slight smile curved her lips.

"Now that the dress is settled, on to the next item on the agenda." Shiela said. "I have been craving Eugene's since we got here, so Paul and I are going tonight before we get too busy with the wedding. I wondered if you two want to go with us."

"Yes." The word was out of Wayne's mouth before he could stop it.

Val glanced between the siblings, then landed on Wayne. "I thought you were watching the game with your dad."

"You and your sports." Sheila scoffed. "Are you really going to turn down Eugene's for baseball?"

"I'm sure my dad will understand if I cancel on him."

"Good. Meet us downstairs at five."

When they were alone, Val looked around the suite before motioning to her back. "Do you think you can help me?"

Wayne didn't know how he managed to unlace the dress without smoothing his fingers over her bare back. When the door closed again, he let out a long sigh. A minute later, Val came out wearing the same outfit as earlier.

"Does this mean you will stay?" He hoped she didn't hear the desperation in his voice.

She crossed her arms, her eyes settling on his chest. "I will for Sheila."

The finality of her words hit him harder than if she had spit in his face. "I—" His throat closed up, refusing to let him admit his growing feelings. "Thank you."

The silence between them grew into an insurmountable cavern, keeping them apart. Her lips pressed together in a thin smile. "She's a good person. I don't want to be the reason for her wedding being ruined."

When was gone, he plopped down on the couch, resting his head in his hands. His mind was at war with his heart. He couldn't decide what he feared more, rejection or reciprocation. He struggled to hold on to the carefully curated indifference he'd developed over the last year. The reality of his growing feelings for Val pressed in on him, and he wasn't sure he wanted to fight them anymore.

CHAPTER 19

VALERIE

Val and Wayne rode down the elevator in an uneasy silence. Though their conversation ended with an obvious finality, she felt like she should say something else. But there were no words to articulate just how hurt she'd been when he said he made a mistake by asking her to stay.

The emotional woman having a hard time filtering out the feelings he invoked in her wanted to be angry and stay distant, yet the logical part of her still tried to figure out why he was so upset in the first place. What did he care if she found another person to spend time with? The way he reversed his stance on Eric left her wondering if he was really worried about how others would perceive her if she was caught with someone else.

The door opened to the lobby, and Wayne waited for her to walk out before following behind her. Shiela and Paul were standing near the entryway.

"Shall we?" Paul held out an arm for the ladies to go ahead.

Val hesitated at the rotating doors of death and eyed the normal exit.

"Is something wrong?" Wayne asked.

She was embarrassed to admit her fear. "I don't like those kinds of doors."

"Neither do I." He went to the other exit and held the door open.

Her skin prickled with goosebumps when she felt his hand slide down her back as he followed her outside. It was a simple gesture. Nothing to read into. But she couldn't help the flutter that rippled through her stomach. The sensation grew stronger when his fingers interlocked with hers, and she looked to the side to find him staring at her.

"Come on, you two."

Val tore herself from his gaze and followed Shiela and Paul across the street. The two-block walk was filled with Sheila's excited chatter about the wedding. She confided in her future husband about a few minor details about the decor, and he smiled and nodded, the adoration obvious in his stare. Val found herself smiling at the couple. They were in love. That much was obvious. But the mutual tenderness they shared made her feel a shameful pang of jealousy.

Not wanting to be caught staring, she turned her gaze to the other side of the street. One particular store caught her attention. There were three mannequins in the long picture window wearing beautiful dresses ranging from casual to formal. She made a mental note to stop by before she left, if only to pretend she could pull off such regal dresses.

Her eyes drifted to Wayne, who had his head turned, looking at the same store. "See something you like?"

Averting her gaze to the sidewalk, she shrugged. "Maybe."

"I don't know if anyone told you, but we are going to a ballet in Salt Lake tomorrow night."

Her eyes widened. "Since when?"

"Dad arranged it a while ago. I guess it never came up." He nodded across the street, where the apparel store disappeared out of view. "I can take you shopping so you can find a dress."

Unable to fight the chance to make a dig at him, she said "I thought my wardrobe was fine."

Instead of getting angry, he smiled. "Dinner with the family is one thing, but a ballet is the perfect chance to go all out."

There was no denying the allure dressing up for a night on the town. Then the reality of her financial situation dimmed the excitement. "I doubt I can afford anything in there."

He opened his mouth to say something, but Sheila dragged her forward. "Did I hear someone say shopping?"

Val got as far as a single syllable before Wayne spoke. "I thought I would take Val to find a dress for the ballet," Wayne said.

The fact that Val hadn't agreed to go with him didn't seem to make a difference.

Sheila raised a brow. "You? I don't think so. It's the perfect opportunity for us girls to have a girl's day. It will give Val a chance to meet the other bridesmaids."

Val shot Wayne a tilted smile. "I guess I'm going shopping with your sister."

The warm light shining on the sidewalk invited them to partake in the homemade pasta sauce and fresh baked bread smell drifting from the closed door. They hadn't taken two steps into the small dining room when a tall, blond-haired woman backed out of a swinging door, holding a tray of food.

As soon as she spotted the newcomers, her whole face lit up, accentuating the icy depths of her blue eyes. "I was beginning to think you weren't coming by."

Sheila matched her smile. "I couldn't wait until the wedding to eat your food."

"Take a seat wherever you like. I'll be around in a minute with menus."

There was an empty table for four near the long window overlooking the main street through town. Sheila and Paul took the chairs facing the front door, while Val and Wayne sat opposite them with a view of the back wall with a hand-painted mural of a scenic little village nestled in a valley surrounded by lush green mountains.

"You've got to try the veal," Sheila said, pointing to Val's menu. "It is out of this world. Unless, of course, you are a vegan, then your best bet is the grilled veggie panini."

"I am now and always will be a carnivore. Fruits and vegetables have their place. It's just not at the top of my food pyramid."

A round of quiet laughter rippled across the table. Wayne leaned into her, the scent of his cologne filling her senses, leaving her breathless and dizzy. His voice was low, so only she could hear him. "If I remember correctly, you like your wine dark and tart."

A flush of heat ran up her neck and filled out her cheeks, and she brushed a strand of hair behind her ear. "That sounds good."

The woman who greeted them came bouncing over to their table, carrying a handful of menus. She looked over the group, her gaze lingering on Val. "I recognize all of your faces except this beautiful young woman."

Sheila nodded across the table. "Sandy, I'd like you to meet Valerie, Wayne's girlfriend. Val, this is Sandy. She is the single most important person behind this bistro."

Sandy waved a dismissive hand. "You don't give Charles enough credit. He is the life blood of the kitchen."

"Yeah, but you keep him in line."

Turning her attention back to Val, Sandy said, "It's a pleasure to meet you, Valerie. I hope you understand what a handful you have here with Wayne."

Val hated to be put on the spot, but took the comment in stride. "I'm beginning to."

More laughter filled the air, then Sandy set a menu in front of each person at the table. "What can I get you to drink?"

"Val and I will have the Mountain Town Red," Wayne said.

"Oh, that sounds nice," Sheila agreed. "We'll have the same."

Sandy made an approving nod. "Very good choice."

For the rest of the meal, Sheila talked excitedly about the wedding; small changes she made to the floral arrangements, last-minute guest list changes, and having to find someone else to handle the music, since apparently, the D.J. they hired had to back due to scheduling conflicts.

Val was surprised the bride to be wasn't chewing her acrylic nails off. The stark difference between Sheila and Wayne was like night and day. The same thing could be said about Val and her brother, but she always attributed it to the age gap.

When it came time to leave, Val wondered if she would make it back to the resort. She hadn't intended to eat so much, but Paul ordered a tiramisu to split between the four of them, and Val had a weakness for anything creamy and sweet.

Outside, she held back from Sheila and Paul, letting them go ahead. If she didn't want to end up with a stomachache, she needed to help dinner digest a little more.

Wayne noticed her absence beside him and asked, "Is everything alright?"

"It's such a lovely night. I thought I'd take a more scenic route to the resort. Walk off some of the veal and wine."

"Mine if I come along?"

"Sure, why not?" She kept her tone indifferent, not wanting him to hear the excitement in her voice.

They walked in silence for a long time. Val studied the mountains, backlit by thousands of twinkling stars. "It's so surreal here."

Wayne kept the slow pace she set. "Yes, it is. Sometimes, I'm tempted to sell everything I own and buy a tiny cabin in the mountains and just disappear. I could spend the rest of my life staring at these skies."

She let out a wistful sigh. "That sounds amazing. Let me know if you decide to go through with it. I'm a pretty quiet roommate."

Their eyes met and, in the starlight, she was taken aback by his smile reflected in the moonlight. His dimple made her knees weak, and she wanted nothing more than to kiss him under the waning moon.

The voice of reason prodded her better judgment. Did she really want to travel down that road again? If she kissed him, could she go back to their tentative arrangement? The answer was depressingly clear. If she gave in to those desires, she wouldn't be able to lie to herself anymore.

As if sensing her need, he stepped in front of her, their bodies nearly touching. Her heart pounded against her chest, anticipating his next move. He watched her, waiting for permission. All she had to do was move into him, just a little, and he would kiss her. Even if her mind begged her back to away, her traitorous body fell in league with her heart and leaned into him.

He brought his hand to her face, but instead of kissing her, he pressed his lips against her forehead. The tender show of endearment matched the smile on his face, but a pang of disappointment bit into her chest. Maybe she misread him. What if it was his way of nicely turning her down?

With the moment passed, she eased back and started walking again. The rest of the trek back to the resort held an awkward air between them. He kept his distance, though not enough to say he was avoiding her.

By the time they arrived at the resort, she had convinced herself he saved her from making another stupid mistake by rejecting her advance. Their roles were set in stone and no matter how much she may have wanted to explore something more, Wayne's actions made it clear how he felt about her.

After closing himself off in the bathroom, she went to her suitcase where she'd shoved the camera. Given how their night ended, she wondered when or if another opportunity would present itself to give it to him. Before she could talk herself out of it, she set the bag on the table.

CHAPTER 20

WAYNE

WAYNE WAS STILL STARING at the ceiling when the sun began cresting the distant mountains. From his position on the couch, he could see the sky bloom into pastel pinks and purples of the coming dawn. The last time he glanced at his phone, it had been a little after five. He'd been tempted to wake Val and ask her if she wanted to trek up the trail and watch the sunrise.

When he walked out of the shower last night, he found a bag on the table. As soon as he saw the logo of the antique store in town, he felt like someone had punched him in the gut. It was the same packaging she'd been holding yesterday when he made a fool of himself over Eric.

The same fool that blew the perfect chance of redeeming himself. There was no question Val wanted him to kiss her. Her eyes, lips and body begged him to. And God did he want to.

But he knew if he did, they would end up in bed together. As much as he yearned to be with her again, he wanted to show her just how much she meant to him; that it wasn't only her body he desired. The disappointment on her face when he kissed her forehead was excruciating. Afterward, he didn't have the balls to try to reclaim the moment.

From his place on the hide-a-bed, he heard her phone ding throughout the night with incoming texts. They lasted until well into the early morning, which told him he wasn't the only one having a hard time sleeping.

Unable to lie there any longer, he got up and called down to the front desk to request the same coffee spread as yesterday and ordered them something to eat. He had a feeling they would both need the caffeine to make it through the day. Just after he got off the phone with room service, his phone buzzed. Sheila's name popped up, followed by a quick text asking if he was up.

He typed out a one-word reply and took the phone with him to the bedroom door. He was torn between knocking, possibly waking Val, and sneaking inside to grab his clothes so she could sleep. Both options weren't ideal, so he decided to throw on the shirt and jeans from last night and stepped out onto the balcony to enjoy the quiet morning.

Sheila texted again. Tell Val I'll be by in an hour.

Will do.

He set the phone down on the glass table in between the two chairs on the balcony. From the corner of his eye, he saw a figure pass by the open doors, into the kitchen. Val took out a coffee pod from the drawer underneath the Keurig.

"I ordered us breakfast," he said. "And coffee."

She paused for a second, and he thought she would continue to make her coffee. He relaxed when she set the pod back in its place, then went to the fridge for a bottle of water instead.

Wayne stood at the bar dividing the kitchenette and living space. "Sheila texted. She will be here in an hour." He reached into his back pocket, drawing out his wallet. When he tried to hand her his credit card, she stared at it like it was going to bite her.

"What's that for?"

"Your dress."

Rolling her eyes, she said, "I have my own money."

"I know, but you weren't expecting to have such a big expense. You shouldn't be on the hook for our plans."

"If I didn't have the funds, I wouldn't go."

He searched her face and eyes for any semblance of the spark of desire from last night. A knock on the door drew her attention away.

She moved around him. "That must be breakfast."

Wayne exhaled sharply, running a hand through his hair. She opened the door to the room-service attendant, who wheeled in a cart laden with their breakfast and coffee. The rich aroma filled the room, but it did little to distract Wayne from the knot of emotions twisting in his chest. He waited until they were alone to wheel the car to the table. Val sat down, taking two cups from the tray next to the carafe and filling them both.

He stared at the credit card in his hand, then set it down beside her. "I don't care how much it costs. Find a dress you love." He started for the bedroom.

"Aren't you going to eat?" She eyed the card next to her.

"I will after I shower." He paused at the door. "Thank you for the camera."

Keeping her back to him, she shrugged. "It's nothing fancy. I don't know if you like those kinds of things." She turned her head to the side, catching his gaze.

"It was very thoughtful. I love it."

Behind the closed door of the bathroom, he slumped against the cold wood. "I love you," he whispered. The words felt foreign on his tongue, but they were true all the same.

CHAPTER 21

VALERIE

VAL WAS GLAD WAYNE hadn't finished with his shower by the time Sheila came by. Not wanting to offend him again, she grabbed his credit card and put it in her wallet with no intention of using it. Hearing him express his appreciation for her stupid little gift made her feel a little better about things.

Sheila waited in the hall. "Morning sunshine. Prepare yourself for a full day of fun and shopping."

"I am looking forward to it," Val said, and she really meant it. The thought of getting out of the resort and away from the tense environment thrilled her.

Sheila spent the fifteen second ride downstairs texting with someone. On the ground floor, she said, "Mandi and Elanor are meeting us in the lobby." She frowned at her phone. "I guess Michelle is staying with her fiancé."

As soon as the door opened, Rita was there, waiting to step inside. Her eyes locked onto Val and her sharp features tightened. She stood her ground, forcing Val to take a step to the side. Sheila wasn't intimidated and brushed past her, drawing a pointed stare from Rita.

"Having a girl's day?" Rita asked.

"Yes, we are," Sheila answered, drawing Val back. "And why are you still here? Did you seriously think I was going to ask you to be in my wedding?"

Val glanced between the women, trying to figure out if their acidic smiles would turn to blows.

Rita's pinched features softened when she laughed. "I'm here as Jennifer's guest." She cut her eyes to Val for a split second.

"Too bad this isn't her wedding. Consider your invitation rescinded." Sheila dismissed Rita by turning away from her. To Val, she said, "Don't worry about her. Daddy and Paul are going to take Wayne golfing while we are gone."

At the fountain, two other women joined them. After a quick round of hugs, Sheila said, "Val, I'd like you to meet my good friends, Eleanore and Mandi."

Mandi's eyes slid down and up Val's body, but her smile wasn't malicious. "So you're the woman who's captured Wayne's wandering eye."

"Be nice," Shiela warned.

Mandi flipped a lock of Val's hair off her shoulder. "I didn't mean anything by it. I'm glad he's finally over that horrid heifer."

"For real," Eleanore agreed.

They opted to walk to the boutique since it wasn't far from the resort. Val felt like a fourth wheel. Sheila and the other women did most of the talking. Mostly jumping from one topic to another with the ease of people who'd been friends for years, leaving Val on the outside looking in.

At the boutique, Shiela was immediately greeted by an older woman with sleek silver hair pulled into a sophisticated updo. "I wondered if you were going to stop by."

"You know how it is. All this wedding planning is more than I bargained for." Shiela and the shop owner exchanged a brief hug. "I should have hired someone to deal with everything."

The woman nodded. "It's not for the weak, that's for sure."

Motioning to Val, Sheila said, "Helen, this is Valerie. She needs a new dress for the ballet tonight."

Helen dragged Val from one rack to another, muttering under her breath and picking out a few dresses. "I think this is a good start. The fitting room is in the back."

"I want to see them on you," Shiela said.

Val took her handful of dresses and chose an empty stall. The first one she put on wasn't something she would have chosen on her own. The pale blue dress hugged her curves a little tighter than she liked. She stepped outside the curtain, frowning.

All four women looked her over, eyes narrowed.

"No," Mandi said, shooing her back inside. "It's the wrong color."

Val got much the same reactions for each of the other dresses and was ready to back out altogether when Elanor pushed a dress inside the curtain. "I found it. The perfect dress."

Val stared at the green fabric. She met her gaze in the mirror, looking over the beautiful dress. It reminded her of the one she'd worn on the night of the date, and a flutter of regret rippled through her. The weight of the lie she and Wayne had devised began to crush her conscience. She hated deceiving Shiela.

"You okay in there?" Mandi asked.

Giving herself a mental shake, Val joined the other women.

A murmur of approval rumbled between them. Helen stepped forward and adjusted the straps.

"Oh yes." Elanor said. "When Wayne sees you in that dress, he won't be able to think about another woman."

Helen smiled. "It is a perfect fit."

Val looked over her visage one last time, frowning at her unimpressive curves and breasts. One look at her in the dress and Wayne would probably have a hard time keeping the disappointment off his face. But this night wasn't just about him. Val decided she would make the best of her situation.

Before she could talk herself out of it, she changed back into her boring clothes and hung the dress on its hanger. At the register, she pulled out her wallet, and Shiela said, "It's already taken care of."

"I can pay for my own dress."

"Don't worry. I'll get money out of Wayne later."

Val eyed the other woman, wondering if he called Sheila about the credit card. Deciding it wasn't worth the fight, she smiled. "Thank you."

"Now, let's grab a bite to eat before heading back."

CHAPTER 22

WAYNE

WAYNE STOOD IN FRONT of a mirror near the kitchenette, trying to figure out his tie. Despite living on his own for nearly a decade, he hadn't quite perfected the art of the perfect Windsor knot. His fingers fumbled through the motions, each flip and tuck frustrating him more and more until he yanked the tie from around his neck and muttered a quick curse.

After spending the day with his dad and future brother-in-law, Wayne returned to the suite and fidgeted with the camera. Despite its age, with a little TLC, he could get it into working order. He couldn't wait to show Val some of the pictures he would take with it. Then reality came crashing in on him, and he knew he would probably never have the chance to do so. Once the wedding was over, there would be no reason for them to stay in each other's lives.

The bedroom door opened and Val stepped out. She fidgeted with the straps of her dress, then smoothed the fabric at her midsection. Wayne looked from her hands to the contours of her breasts hugged tight in the silky material like two perfect porcelain—

"Having trouble with your tie?"

Her voice drew his attention from her chest to her face, and he cleared his throat. "Uh, yeah." He went back to his reflection. "I've never been able to do it right."

"Here." Val reached for him, and it was all he could do not to flinch from the electricity of her touch. "Been a few years, but it's like riding a bike. You never quite forget how to do it." Her smile was faint and introspective. "I used to do this for my dad. I'd lay them out, one for each day of the week. My mom didn't have the dexterity or the patience, so he taught me."

Instead of watching her hands deftly make a perfect Windsor, he was mesmerized by the way she tucked her bottom lip in her upper teeth as she concentrated on her work. Her eyes slid back and forth, matching the movements of her fingers. Her nostrils flared ever so slightly when she tightened the knot.

"It's not really fair."

Her fingers paused and when she cut her gaze up to his, the pounding in his chest intensified.

"I've told you a lot about my family," he blurted. "But other than the brother you mentioned, I don't know anything about yours."

Going back to the tie, she gave him a slight shrug. "There's not much to tell. My dad is an insurance adjuster. My mom works part time at an animal shelter. Rob, my brother, is in the process of finishing his master's in business finance. After their third child was born, he took some time off from college to pursue a better-paying job to help with their growing family."

"No dark family secrets?"

Again, her stare made breathing a struggle. She pursed her lips together and said, "It's not so much a secret, but a sinister rumor started by a jilted lover. One of my aunts supposedly killed her first husband because he was an abusive alcoholic and beat her on a regular basis. My mom says it's far from the truth. Apparently, the man died from liver failure, according to the coroner's report. Then again, it's also rumored my aunt slept with the coroner to make the evidence of foul play disappear."

"What do you think happened?"

"Aunt June never denied it, but I think that's because she wanted to keep people out of her business. She is a very private person." Val patted his tie and cocked her head to the side. "That looks pretty good, don't you think?" When he didn't answer immediately, her smile faded. "I'm sure you can find someone to fix it for you."

"No. It's perfect. Thank you."

He saw a hint of pink color her cheeks, and she grabbed a small purse from the table. "I guess we should head downstairs." She reached the door, and he still hadn't moved. Glancing over her shoulder, she said, "Is something wrong?"

He shook his head. "The dress. It looks beautiful on you."

She ran a hand over her neck. "Come on."

The ride downstairs was awkward and silent. A few times, Wayne went to take her by the hand, but the argument they'd had earlier still lingered in his mind, so he kept his hands tucked behind his back. When the doors opened, Shiela and Paul were already waiting in the lobby.

As soon as his sister saw them, her mouth split into a wide smile. "Oh my God, Valerie, you look gorgeous."

Val's head dropped, trying to hide her embarrassed smile.

Wayne searched the rest of the lobby. "Where's Mom and Dad?"

"They are meeting us at the venue. Paul and I rented a limo for the evening so we can travel in style."

He noticed Val lift her head, unafraid to show her excited smile that time. "Shall we go, then?" he said.

Sheila and Paul settled into the seat farther from the doors, so Wayne and Val slid into the free seat. Val kept a few inches between them, staring at the scenery passing by. She was doing that thing where she twisted the fabric of her dress with her fingers, and he smiled to himself, wondering if she knew just how adorable she was.

"After the show, we have reservations at Nicolina's," Shiela said to Val. "The view from the rooftop bar is spectacular."

"Sounds fancy," Val mused, turning a cheeky grin on Wayne. "I'm going to be spoiled by all these fancy shows and dinners. I'll never want to eat at a fast-food joint again."

Shiela laughed. "Trust me. It gets old really quick. I'd rather stuff my face with a greasy cheeseburger and fries than a bite sized portion of some dish I can't even pronounce."

Paul brought the back of her hand to his lips. "God, I love that about you. My wallet does too."

Wayne glanced to the side where Val watched his sister and future husband. The smile on her face didn't reach her eyes. Even in the dim light of the limo, he could see the longing sparkling in those hazel depths. Without thinking, he reached to the right and rested his hand on hers. He felt her fingers twitch, but she didn't pull away. Instead, she moved her thumb up over his pinky, sweeping it back and forth, sending tiny bolts of electricity up his arm.

Never in his life did he wish so badly to travel into the past. Only a week or so, to give him the chance to turn down Lisa's proposal and seek out Valerie on his own. Would she have given him the time of day if he simply approached her? There was no doubt about the undeniable attraction and chemistry they shared.

But the past was set in stone. Now, he had to forge ahead, and watch an amazing woman pretend to be his girlfriend, only to eventually lose her again.

CHAPTER 23

VALERIE

Val's door opened, and an older man wearing a neatly pressed, dark mahogany suit held out a hand to her. His brimmed hat sat atop salt and pepper hair, highlighting the bright hue of his brown eyes that were accented with deep laugh lines as he smiled. He helped her out of the back seat, and she hadn't gotten two steps when Wayne encased her waist with an arm. Her first instinct was to sidle out of his reach, but the feel of him by her side was too comforting to abandon just yet.

Shiela and Paul joined them at the set of four tall glass doors. She craned her neck to peek over the other guests, then pulled out her cellphone. "I'll text Jennifer. Dad probably left his phone at the resort."

"We can wait for them inside," Paul said, opening a door for them.

It took a concerted effort for Val not to stare, open-mouthed, at the old-world beauty of the lobby. Had she not known they were in the modern world, she could imagine herself being transported back decades ago when such opulence was the norm. Gold gilded virtually every piece of decor. The glass like finish of the marble floor practically glowed with the warmth of the place. Ahead of them lay a grand staircase, carpeted in a dark, rich maroon fabric she was scared to walk on.

Wayne's hand squeezed her hip, urging her to move with them through the crowd, where they found an empty space to loiter without being in anyone's way.

"They are pulling up now." Shiela dropped her phone in the tiny clutch, matching her simple cream-colored gown.

Val turned her attention to the entrance, watching for them. For the second time since arriving in Utah, she thought her mind was playing tricks on her. Along with Greg and Jennifer, another woman followed them inside.

"What the hell is she doing here?" Shiela's voice was just above a whisper.

Wayne's arm fell from where it had rested above Val's hips, and she looked over to see him staring at Rita. All she could focus on was the way his jaw went slack, and a quick, but powerful contraction of his throat made his Adam's apple bob up and down.

Shiela took a step forward, but Paul wrapped an arm around her waist. "Don't make a scene. You can unleash your wrath at the resort."

She pursed her lips, her pristine, manicured brows stitching together. Then she looked over her shoulder at Val, who quickly averted her eyes to the floor. Val didn't want the other woman to see just how uncomfortable she was with the situation. There was no reason for it, after all. She knew perfectly well Wayne still harbored feelings for Rita. But did he have to flaunt it in front of everyone?

Greg reached them before Jennifer and Rita, who had stopped by some other guests to chat. "I'm sorry, Shiela, I tried to tell Jen this was a bad idea, but she'd already bought Rita's ticket."

"I'll let this go, for now. Your wife is one shenanigan away from being banned from my wedding."

Val stopped listening. She used the distraction as a chance to sneak away to compose herself. A sign directed her to the lady's restroom, and that was the perfect place for her to have a few minutes to herself.

Luckily, only a few women lingered in the bathroom, and they were wrapped up in their own conversations, so Val snuck past the single, long mirror that made up most of the wall in front of the sinks. She stuffed herself in the farthest stall from the door and sat down on the toilet seat. Her stomach clenched, and she wanted to scream her frustrations out into the echoing chamber of the stall. Instead, she rested her head on the base of her palms, careful not to mess up the makeup she'd spent over half an hour to perfect.

She heard the outer bathroom door open, and a pair of heels clacked across the marble floor at a slow, steady pace before stopping in front of her stall.

"You okay in there?" Shiela's voice was somehow comforting, even though Val dreaded the idea of talking to anyone.

Val lifted her head and forced a smile, hoping it would come through in her voice. "Yeah, I'll be right out. I shouldn't have had that last bottle of water." She stood, flushed the unused toilet, and unlatched the door.

Shiela had gone to the row of porcelain sinks and ran her hands under the gold faucets. She watched Val approach, her expression frustratingly hard to gage. A family trait passed down from Greg, no doubt.

"Did Wayne say something to you?"

Val kept her eyes glued to the stream of water. "What? No. I told you, I just had to—"

"Cut the bullshit, Valerie."

Val met the other woman's stare in the mirror. "He didn't say anything. He didn't have to."

A twitch of emotion flickered over Shiela's face, and she shook her hands over the sink before grabbing a few paper towels from the nearby dispenser, handing one to Val. "Can I let you in on a little secret?"

Val's hand rested on the tap as she stared at Sheila.

"Wayne was one of the biggest reasons I tolerated living at home for as long as I did. I watched him grow from this tiny annoying bratty brother to a kind, thoughtful, and sometimes annoying young man. I was there for his first heartbreak when he was still in high school." She rested a hand on the counter so she could lean into Val.

"I had moved out by the time he and Rita started dating, but we talked almost every day. We were each other's anchors in the tumultuous shit show that is our family. I was the only one he told about the engagement ring. She broke up with him before he had the chance to propose."

"Why did she break things off?" Val asked.

"Who knows? She just woke up one day and sent him a Dear John text saying she felt smothered and needed to find herself. Ghosted the whole family."

"Why are you telling me this?"

"Because I want you to understand that whatever you think you saw on Wayne's face just now is not some deep-seated subconscious desire to get back together with her."

Val shook her head, but Shiela cut off her next thought.

"I know because I was there when he fell apart. She broke him and he hasn't been the same person since. Until now. I see how he looks at you. When you two are together, I glimpse the old, happier Wayne."

Their conversation should have eased the aching inside Val, but it only compounded the guilt that ate at her because of the lie she and Wayne had concocted. "Shiela, I need to tell you something. Wayne and I—"

Shiela's phone dinged, and she rolled her eyes. "The show is about to start and the guys are freaking out about how we are going to make them late. We can finish our little chat later, okay?"

"Yeah. Okay."

Val followed her out of the bathroom, fighting to keep her face from pinching into a scowl. She didn't see Wayne at first. Gregory and Paul were standing near a life size painting of a group of ballerinas enacting the ending scene of Swan Lake.

Someone grabbed her arm, and she slowed to a stop, turning to find Wayne staring at her, concern etched into his chiseled appearance. "Are you alright?"

She worked up one side of her mouth. "Of course. I guess I forgot to tell you I inherited my mom's micro bladder."

Though his expression relaxed, his eyes never left hers. "When we get back to the resort, I want us to talk."

By some divine intervention, Val managed to keep the horrified, gut clenching feeling from showing on her face. At least she didn't think it did, by the way Wayne didn't react. "Sure. Is everything okay?" She even impressed herself when her voice remained steady.

What he did next left her even more stupefied. He cupped the side of her face and pressed his lips to hers for a brief kiss. When he pulled back, he smiled. "I hope so. I mean, I want it to be."

There was so much she wanted to say, to ask, but the only word she seemed to remember in her vast vocabulary was, "Alright."

He moved his arm into hers and led her to where the others waited to go into the venue.

CHAPTER 24

WAYNE

Wayne couldn't concentrate on the show. His thoughts were preoccupied with the woman sitting beside him. Once the lights dimmed and the dancers took the stage, Val's full attention never wavered from the beautifully choreographed dance. She shifted in her seat, her breath matching the ebb and flow of the ballerinas.

When she disappeared after his parents showed up with Rita in tow, he thought she might have actually left the venue and grabbed a cab and left. But Paul had seen her disappear into the lady's restroom. He'd been relieved, and at the same time furious. Not at Val, though. His mother lacked boundaries when it came to his life. It had been that way since birth. Jennifer had a reputation to uphold and expected her son to follow in her footsteps. If not for his dad, Wayne would have gone insane.

The only reason he ever agreed to go out with Rita was the fact that she'd been the only daughter of a high-profile lawyer who happened to be good friends with his mom's side of the family. The first time he met Rita, he made up his mind she was so incredibly wrong for him. After a couple of dates away from the pressure of both their families, they actually hit it off.

Rita had been as ambitious as she was beautiful. In the beginning of their relationship, she had been incredibly attentive and genuine. That attention made it easy to overlook their lack of shared interests. After she broke off their relationship, he tried to pinpoint what went wrong. It was Rita's last year of law school. She hadn't changed, really. There were times they would go days without talking, but they made up for it over holiday and summer breaks.

After she sent him the text, ending their six-year relationship, he shut himself off from everyone. A part of him wished she had cheated, but everyone in her family insisted she had been faithful until the end. She just stopped loving him. If she ever did in the first place.

It had been a fluke, his career in the escort business. For months after the breakup, he spent most of his time in bars, until one night, an older woman approached him and offered him a hefty sum to go back to her hotel room. He would have slept with her for free, but she insisted on paying him. After that night, he began getting referrals.

Apparently, he wasn't that good of an escort because, less than a year into it, he met Val. The reality of the closed off, lonely existence threatened to crumble and bury him under the rubble.

Val shifted beside him, leaning forward in anticipation of the finale. He studied her profile. Her lips parted as she drew in a breath. The swell of her chest distracted him, but only for a second. The spell was broken when Rita stood up and made a point to sidestep toward them, despite being only a few seats from the other end. Val's eyes flicked upward, but she leaned over so as not to miss the last few minutes of the ballet.

Rita slowed her pace before stopping in front of Wayne and tried to brush a hip against him, but he leaned back, making the same maneuver as Val, and pretended to watch the finale. From his periphery, he could see Rita standing in the aisle, as if waiting for him to follow. It occurred to him then, even if he was there alone, having not met Val, he still wouldn't entertain the idea of pursuing Rita. Her cruel dismissal of their relationship had killed any feelings he had for her. Any semblance of regret was for the memory of what they had. Of what would never be again.

They remained in their seats for a while after the show ended, letting the crowd thin out. Wayne stood, holding out his hand to Val. He relaxed when she took it and let him lead her up the carpeted aisle. He was tempted to break away and demand his dad take his mom and Rita back to the resort so they wouldn't have to put up with the drama. His stomach knotted as he waited for his parents to come through, then Val stepped into his line of sight and nodded past him.

"If you're looking for Rita, she's over there." She nodded to the archway leading to the restrooms.

He felt the frown pulling at his mouth deepen. "I wasn't looking for her."

Val shrugged and crossed her arms. "I think she expected you to follow her earlier."

"So what if she did? I have nothing else to say to her. I'm here with you." She opened her mouth to speak again, and he snapped, "I am not interested in getting back with Rita. How many times do I have to say it out loud for you and the rest of my family to get it?"

Her eyes went wide and her body visibly tensed. He wanted to gobble up the words before they reached her ears, but it was too late. Shame made him spin around and head for the front door. It took every ounce of will power not to turn around, but he couldn't bear to see the look on her face.

CHAPTER 25

VALERIE

THE DRIVE TO NICOLINA'S was made in excruciating silence. Every time Sheila tried to talk, Wayne cut her off with a hard stare. Val was at a loss for words. She should be furious with him for the way he spoke to her, but she had been purposefully snarky, and it bit her in the ass.

Wayne had every right to be angry. There were a couple of times she wanted to reach for his hand, like he had done on the ride to the ballet. The thought of his rejection kept her arm planted in her lap, clutching the purse.

Upon their arrival at the restaurant, Wayne still wasn't talking to anyone, but he did hold the door for Val. The meal was even more awkward since, of course, Rita had to join them. Gregory and Paul did their best to keep the conversation light and fun. Sheila didn't attempt to try to hide her disdain for certain guests at the table, which Val found quite satisfying.

Val took the first opportunity to excuse herself, making her way to the glass balcony surrounding the seating area. She wished she'd brought her sketchbook so she could capture the beauty of the city lights silhouetting the distant mountains. The sky sparkled with diamond-like stars, accented by the waning moon. She closed her eyes, implanting the scene into her mind's eye for later.

"You realize you are just a passing fling."

The sound of Rita's musical voice made Val's stomach drop. She opened her eyes, choosing to focus on the moon rather than the other woman.

"Wayne and I were made for each other."

Pushing out a breathy laugh, Val said, "Is that why you ghosted him?"

"I had my reasons."

Val rolled her eyes. "If you say so."

She could feel Rita inching closer. "You're a fool if you think you will ever be accepted into this family. It doesn't matter how many women he dates, all roads lead back to me."

Val looked away from the view, meeting the other woman's stare. "So go get him."

Rita blinked at her, the smug smile faltering. "Excuse me?"

She pointed to where the men stood at the bar waiting for drinks. "If you think he is yours for the taking, march your prissy ass on over there and take him back." She pushed past Rita, disappearing into an isolated dark corner of the seating area.

Despite Wayne insisting he didn't harbor feelings for Rita, Val understood the allure of returning to the comfort of someone you gave so much of yourself to.

The sound of heavy footsteps brought her out of her pitiful thoughts, and she turned in time to see Wayne's anger glowing in the warm light of the propane heaters.

"Did you tell Rita she could have me?"

"Something like that, yeah."

"What the hell, Valerie? I'm not some object to be passed around from one woman to another."

She cocked her head to the side and crossed her arms.

He held up a hand. "You know what I mean."

Resisting the urge to travel down that road, she said, "Apparently, Rita is under the impression you will eventually come around and take her back. So, I told her to go for it."

He opened his mouth to reply, but she cut him off.

"Because if we were really dating, it would be under the assumption of trust. I wouldn't have to question your loyalty and commitment to our supposed relationship. If I had that kind of trust in you, there would be no reason to worry about your ex fiancé swooping in and winning you back."

Sucking in a sharp breath, she made herself go on. "If you were by yourself, I think there is a part of you who would have considered getting back together with her. Right or wrong, you were with her for a long time. I think deep down, you miss it. You miss her." The visage of his face blurred despite her best efforts to keep her emotions in check. "Because if Thomas had come to me asking for a second chance, I would have probably given it to him. No matter how much he hurt me, I miss the people we used to be together."

"That's just it, Val. I'm not that man anymore. You aren't that woman. If I was by myself, I still wouldn't want Rita back. And I'd like to think you wouldn't forgive Thomas for the awful things he did to you. We may be pretending about us, but I would never purposefully hurt you like that. For the sake of this week and the wedding, you are the only woman in my life." He held on to her gaze, and for a harrowing few seconds, she thought he was going to say more. Hoped he would say more. But he simply turned and walked away.

As soon as he disappeared around the corner, she spun in a circle, feeling trapped. There was nowhere to run or hide, and she badly needed to get away from everyone. Especially Wayne.

She shoved at the tears that had broken the dam of her lashes and pulled out a tissue from her purse to blot any running mascara. It took her a few minutes to compose herself and hopefully let her eyes de-puff so no one would suspect she'd been crying.

Years of shoving her feelings down into her gut paid off. By the time she made it back to the bar area, she even managed to put on a fake smile. Sheila studied her for a few seconds, but if she suspected anything, she didn't let it show. Wayne nursed a beer next to his dad at the bar. He glanced over his shoulder and Val averted her eyes before he caught her staring. The bright spot was the absence of Rita. Val tried to make a casual show of looking over the thinning crowd, but she was nowhere to be seen.

Val took comfort in the knowledge that Wayne was, for the most part, over Rita. The flip side was his contentment in the life he'd made for himself after their breakup. One that involved meaningless nights with other women who paid him to be a fantasy. Something she would have never considered doing on her own. Now, though, the thought of hiring a complete stranger to ease her loneliness, even for one night at a time, was better than the alternative.

She had to accept their roles as pretend lovers. She glanced to the side where Wayne watched her and softened her features, smiling at him. On the inside, her heart was already breaking.

CHAPTER 26

WAYNE

WAYNE DIDN'T EVEN TASTE the food on his plate. The steady buzz of conversation around him felt like static in his head, and the only thing he could focus on was the tension radiating off Val. She fingered the delicate stem of the wineglass in front of her, pretending to be engrossed in something Sheila said. The more she purposefully avoided his gaze, the more agitated it made him. He was still angry at how flippant Val had been with Rita regarding him.

He hadn't planned to eavesdrop when he saw the two women talking. It was pure coincidence, or so he told himself, that he was close enough to hear the tail end of the exchange.

Then go get him.

Val's words had struck him like a slap to the face. The irony wasn't lost on him, though. Hadn't he been as cruel with the way he spoke to her at the venue? He couldn't blame her for being so angry? He studied her profile, amazed at how in control of her emotions she appeared to be. No one would have guessed she'd been crying just minutes earlier.

One bright spot in the evening was Rita's absence, setting him more at ease. Apparently, she took the hint and left. His mom scowled at her wine, ignoring everyone around her. His dad caught his attention and shot him a quick wink. It was rare for Greg McNab to put his foot down with his wife, but when he did, Jennifer usually backed down.

Despite the absence of a certain proverbial thorn in his side, the dinner was already tainted. What was supposed to be a lovely evening to celebrate Sheila and Paul turned out to be one of the most awkward and disappointing nights of Wayne's life. When it came time to leave, there was a collective sense of relief that passed over the entire table. Val still wasn't talking to him, and no matter how badly he craved the feel of her hand in his, he didn't dare touch her.

The drive back was excruciatingly silent. Val hugged the opposite side of the seat as Wayne, staring out the window. Paul nestled Sheila in the crook of his arm, sending a pang of longing and regret through Wayne who wished he could do the same with Val. by the time the limousine pulled under the awning of the resort, he made up his mind about his next move. No matter the outcome, he had to confess his feelings for her. He couldn't let another day pass with the weight of unsaid words crush him.

At the elevator, Sheila and Paul stayed back. "I think Paul and I are going to enjoy a quiet walk in the gardens. Don't forget, rehearsal is tomorrow at six. Val, can you join the girls and I about an hour early so we can finish setting up?"

"Of course. I'd love to help." Val seemed genuinely excited.

In the elevator, her lips fell into something not quite a frown, but far from the radiant smile he loved to see on her. She kept herself close to the doors, ready to sprint out as soon as they opened. He kept his pace slow, letting her get inside before him.

She went straight for the bedroom, but paused at the door. "Do you mind if I get in the shower first?"

"Not at all."

He stood beside the table, waiting until he heard the shower come on. It took him another minute or so to work up the courage to step inside the bedroom. He paced back and forth in front of the bed, trying to put his jumbled thoughts and feelings into a coherent sentence. He knew what he wanted to say, but every time he thought about actually speaking the words out loud, his stomach rolled and twisted, and he broke out into a clammy sweat.

Frustrated, He plopped down in the chair near the door. One certainty kept creeping into his mind. He was running out of time. If he didn't tell her now, he would never get the chance again.

CHAPTER 27

VALERIE

THE STING OF THE pelting drops helped take Val's mind off the previous few hours. She moved her head from side to side, letting the water cascade down her body, leaving her skin bright red in its wake. She took her time drying off while contemplating her next move once she returned to New Mexico.

She'd been tossing around the idea of moving again. After she and Thomas broke up, she realized their lives were too connected with mutual friends and places they both like to hang out. Hopefully, Lisa would understand. She had to. Maybe she would be open to going with Val.

But leaving her life in New Mexico meant starting all over. The unfairness of it all made her want to scream. Why should she have to be the one to give up yet another aspect of her life? Then there was the question of where she would go. The only logical option was to go back to Texas and admit to her mom and dad they were right. She couldn't run away from her problems forever. She didn't have the money to keep her afloat until she found another job.

A knock jolted her back to the present, and she realized she'd been standing in front of the mirror, staring into the past.

"You almost done?"

"Be right out." She threw on her cotton pajama top and shorts and stepped into the bedroom. Wayne waited beside the door. "All yours."

He didn't move. "Are you okay?"

"Yeah. Why wouldn't I be?" She grabbed the book off the night-stand so she would have something to focus on other than him.

She felt his stare, and it made her uncomfortable, so she latched on to the irritation and glared at him. "What is your problem? I told you, I'm fine. I thought you wanted the shower."

His jaw flexed a few times, but he didn't take his eyes off her. "Can I ask you a question?"

Leaning into her snark again, she said, "That's all you've done so far, so why not another one."

He huffed out an irritated sigh. "Never mind. It's impossible to talk to you when you're like this."

The book dropped from her face. "What the hell is that supposed to mean? Like what?"

"Like this." He waved a hand at her. "Broody and intentionally aloof. Are you really going to pretend like we didn't have that conversation at the restaurant?"

"You made it abundantly clear you had nothing else to say when you ignored me all night."

"I didn't want to continue discussing our situation in front of everyone."

She closed the book, gently laying it on her lap. "Oh, our situation. Okay, Wayne. What do you want to discuss about our situation? Am I not playing my part good enough? Do I need to be more attentive? I'm sorry I don't have a lot of practice pretending to be someone I'm not." She regretted the comment as soon as it rolled past her tongue.

She released a sharp grunt. "I can't do this anymore."

Whatever anger gathered behind his eyes dissipated into confusion.

"We aren't even a real couple, yet here we are bickering like we've been married for decades, refusing to admit when one of us is wrong." She screamed at herself to shut her mouth before she said something she couldn't undo, but her tongue had a mind of its own and wouldn't be sated until it confessed everything.

"Of course I'm broody and aloof. It's my defense mechanism. When I agreed to stay, I was under the assumption I'd be bunking with the guy I met on our date. I thought you would at least pretend to be that guy, anyway."

She stood, letting the book fall to the mattress beside her. "But no. You had to show me the real you. Someone who is even better than first date Wayne. I wanted so badly for you to be this egotistical schmuck who is way too into himself. You couldn't even do that right. So now I'm stuck sharing a room and fake relationship with a man who is actually kind of great. He's smart and charming and—" She closed her eyes and pushed out a breath. "And everything I didn't realize I was looking for."

When she opened her eyes again, Wayne disappeared through the door. She sunk to the bed, groaning to herself. Then the door opened wider, and he came in carrying his pillow.

"What are you doing?"

"What I should have done days ago." He threw the pillow to the other side of the bed. "Taking back my bed."

She stood again and reached for her own pillow.

"Where do you think you're going?"

"To the couch," she said cautiously.

He made three long strides to where she stood, taking her face in his hands, then captured her lips with his. It took her a while for her brain to catch up to her body and when it did, she relaxed into his kiss, wrapping her arms around his neck.

He rested his forehead against hers. "You changed my world the first night we met. I haven't stopped thinking about you since. When you showed up here, it was like fate gave me a second chance." He lifted his head. "I can't keep pretending my feelings for you aren't real, but I'm scared. I made horrible mistakes."

She kissed him again, lingering on the feel of his soft lips. "I don't care about your past. As long as it stays in there." She searched her mind for a way to not sound like she was judging him. "You said yourself the reason you became an escort was to have the financial freedom to step away from your family and their money.

If you give it up now, I don't know if I can stand the thought of being the reason you get sucked back in."

His smile never wavered. "I will sell lemonade on the side of the road if I have to. Even if we went back to our separate lives, I can't go on like I have been. I thought I was prepared for the kind of sacrifice this lifestyle demanded, but I want more than a physical connection. I need someone I can laugh with. Someone I can share my worries with. Someone I can trust. I need...you."

She stared into his eyes, searching for the words to explain the turmoil inside her. Could she ignore his past? Did she want to? What if he decided having a relationship with her wasn't worth giving up the extra income his other life afforded? The uncertainty made her want to wall up her heart and push him away. Yet, she couldn't pretend she didn't care about him. "What do we do now?"

"What we've been doing the whole time, except now, I want us to be the real thing."

Val looked past him, her thoughts on Thomas and the life she had envisioned with him. Now, here she stood, faced with another man who, three years down the road, could betray her too. "If you ever stop caring for me, or you get bored, or just want out, you'll tell me, okay? Don't string me along."

A range of emotions shifted through his face, making the muscles around his eyes and jaw ripple. "I'm not him, Val."

She stared at him, losing herself in his hazel eyes. Finally, she cleared her throat. "I want you to know it's okay to call it quits if something ever changes."

His kiss, though not as forceful as the last, sent her head spinning. He pulled back. "The same goes for you. Despite what you may think, I'm rather vanilla in my everyday life. You've seen my wardrobe."

His brevity was a welcomed distraction from the emotional turmoil still raging inside her. "Good thing I'm a simple woman who has simple needs."

He slid a hand down her side, tucking his fingers into the waistband of her shorts. "And I want to explore every one of those needs. Let me make love to you, Valerie."

There was no universe where she would tell him no. Nor did she want to. She worked her fingers up the base of his neck and into his hair, drawing him into her. His hands gripped her hips before sliding upward, the tips of his fingers leaving a line of fire in their wake.

With one fluid motion, he slipped her shirt over her head. There was no hint of anxiety or shame when he took in her body. The desire burning in his gaze further stoked the blaze running amok inside her veins.

His arms encircled her back, easing her onto the plush duvet, and she had the sensation of being laid on a soft cloud. He urged her legs apart so he could rest between her legs. She reveled in the weight of him on top of her. A hand slid down her outer thigh, pulling her leg up over his hip as he arched into her, dragging a quivering moan from between their lips.

He sat up, slipping her shorts free of her legs. Using one hand, he began the excruciating slow process of unbuttoning his shirt. The other hand moved up her thigh, and using his thumb, teased her like he had their first night together.

She arched into him, keeping her eyes locked on his. To her disappointment, he had to use both hands to finish undressing. He returned to her body, teasing once again before easing inside her, drawing a quivering rasp from her constricted throat.

Through the cloud of ecstasy shadowing her thoughts, there was a brief, worried thought about the lack of protection. But after her previous scare, she had gotten an IUD. She shut out the rest of those nagging voices, embracing the moment. Whatever thoughts might have tried to invade the present were drowned out by the orgasm that rocketed through her. She flung her arms around Wayne's back, his muscles flexing beneath the pressure of her fingers.

Reality faded into the background of the pleasure that consumed her. For an eternity, and a single moment, they were the only two beings left in existence, their bodies moving in sync with one another. Wayne whispered into her ear, his breath hot against her skin. She tried to focus on his words, but they were lost in another quake of thunder rumbling through her.

His movements slowed, and his body trembled with the effort of holding himself above her. They stared at each other, their breathing in synch with the hammering of their hearts.

He caressed her cheek with the back of his fingers. She saw a struggle behind his eyes, but when he smiled, her unease vanished. "I am so happy you came into my life."

Her breath caught in her throat when three words nearly escaped her lips. Dangerous words that shouldn't be in her vocabulary. Not this soon. To keep them inside her, she drew him into a kiss, losing herself in it.

He rolled to the side and scooted to the edge of the bed.

"Where are you going?" Val asked, getting up on her elbow.

His dimpled grin was contagious, and she found herself smiling back at him. "To grab you a washcloth." After a quick pause, he added. "I'm chivalrous like that."

He was gentle when he washed her, and against her will, she wondered if he'd done this for other women, his 'dates'? She tried to keep her smile in place when he looked at her, but she must have failed to do so, because he held her stare for a heartbeat too long.

"This kind of aftercare was not part of the experience."

Her face flushed, and she put a hand over her face. "I don't know how to feel about how easily you can read my mind."

"You don't have the best poker face."

"Still, it's unsettling."

He crawled up her body, his expression irritatingly unreadable. "I am an open book. If you want to know something, all you have to do is ask. I will tell you everything."

She considered his statement. Did she want to know everything? Sometimes, ignorance truly was bliss. Especially when it came to his choice in careers. Relaxing into the pillow, she ran a thumb along his jawline. "I can't promise I won't be insecure sometimes. I mean, I want to trust you; I do trust you." Her chest rose and fell with a long sigh.

He pressed his mouth to each cheek, then the tip of her nose. "It's going to be a big adjustment for us both."

That was the understatement of the year.

"For the time being," he said, pulling back the duvet. "Let's focus on the here and now."

CHAPTER 28

WAYNE

WAYNE WOKE TO THE feel of the sheet shifting on top of his bare chest. He turned his head to the side, peering at the clock on the nightstand. He managed to get a couple of hours of sleep after waking to relieve himself. It had been difficult to sneak out of bed without waking Val. It was even harder not to sidle up to her naked body when he crawled back under the blankets.

Val's movements were small and slight as she eased under the heavy comforter. He let her get settled before rolling over and draping an arm across her chest.

"Sorry," she whispered, resting a hand on his arm. "I didn't mean to wake you."

He brushed his lips against her shoulder. The sweet honey scent of her shampoo filled his senses. "It's okay. We should probably think about getting around if we want to make the summit before sunrise."

She rolled over, the tip of her nose barely touching his. "You actually want to go running?"

"You've inspired me."

Tucking herself deeper into his arms, Val sighed and shimmied against him. "I'm feeling lazy today."

"Oh? Then what are we going to do for cardio?"

"Mm. I think we covered that last night."

The softness of her breasts pressed into him, and he moved a hand down her back, urging her even closer. "There's no reason we can't get another workout in."

She lifted her cheek from his chest. Her smile made his pulse quicken.

He rolled her onto her back, tucking himself between her thighs. He pushed inside her, sucking in a breath when she tightened around him. A pleased moan vibrated against his mouth as he tasted the delicate crevice at the base of her neck.

He moved back ever so slightly. "Unless you're not up for it."

Her response was to dig her fingers into the muscles of his back and bring her legs up, urging him deeper. "Don't you dare stop now."

He pushed up onto his hands to admire her face as he made love to her. He enjoyed the way she bit at her lower lip and her expression shifting with each thrust of his hips. She wasn't afraid to demand each delicious ounce of pleasure, and he was more than happy to fulfill her every desire. Her head tilted back, and she let out a high-pitched moan, lost in her moment of bliss. When she contracted around him, his body took over, unable to stop his own fall into ecstasy.

In the afterglow, they enjoyed the tender caresses of each other's hands and lips. Wayne was reluctant to leave the comfortable warmth of her, and when he moved to the side, his body spasmed one last time.

"I could get used to waking up like this." Val's smile was as wistful and dreamy as her voice.

"You and me both." He kissed her again before climbing out of bed.

"Where are you going?"

"I have a feeling it will take the nectar of the gods to revive you. Plus, I need to make a quick phone call." He put on his boxers and grabbed up his jeans, searching for his phone. When he looked back, she wasn't smiling anymore. "Nothing like that." He turned his attention to the jeans and frowned.

"What's wrong?"

"I can't find my phone. I could have sworn I left it in my pants."

She slid up behind him, the feel of her breasts sending shivers down his spine. "Are you sure you didn't leave it in the limo?"

"I hope not. I'll ask Paul for their information later." He turned in her arms, drawing her into him.

"You can use mine. Just don't go snooping around my Amazon app."

His lips spread into a conspiratory smile.

"As a single woman, I made certain purchases for self-care."

His smile turned to laughter. "Self-care?"

She pushed off him. "A girl's got needs. I'm going to hop into the shower. My phone is on the nightstand."

"I appreciate the offer, but I'll use the phone in the living room. I wouldn't want to be tempted to learn more about your self-care routine."

Her grin threatened to knock him over. After hearing the water turn on, he picked up the phone by the couch and ordered room service. Then he looked through the phonebook and dialed the ranch. Ten minutes later, he'd booked them a full morning on horseback. There was a sense of satisfaction that came with the knowledge he could flaunt his girlfriend in front of Eric.

Wayne stared at the bathroom door.

Girlfriend. He didn't know if that's what they were yet. As scared as he was to leave himself vulnerable again, he couldn't wait to plunge headfirst into a life with Val by his side.

CHAPTER 29

VALERIE

Val was blissfully content from the lavish breakfast Wayne ordered to their room, along with the wonderful way he woke her. Despite the pleasant morning, her circling thoughts threatened to evaporate her good mood as they headed downstairs. No matter how hard she tried to ignore the nagging voices whispering their warnings, by the time they reached the lobby, her body hummed with anxiety.

Last night, while drifting to sleep encased in Wayne's arms, her mind wandered to places she'd rather not have gone. Not yet. She wanted to hang on to the contentment of simply being with him. But she knew eventually they'd have to sit down together and discuss the future. Would he have to find a regular nine-to-five job now he wasn't going to have the extra income? Could her meager salary keep up with the lifestyle he was accustomed to?

They wouldn't move in together right away. She wasn't ready for such a commitment. What if, when Wayne got back to his apartment and had a chance to think about their future relationship, he changed his mind? They didn't know each other that well. Not really. She had certain quirks and expectations in her life incompatible with his lifestyle. From what she saw of his space, he was a neat person, whereas she was prone to letting things slide for a few days until she got around to tidying up.

She mentally shook herself from the rabbit hole of what ifs, and it was then she realized Wayne wasn't beside her. She whirled around, spotting him leaning against the corner of a building a few yards away. He wore a playful smirk on his shadowed face that excited her in ways she didn't expect.

"What are you doing back there?"

"Seeing how long it would take you to realize I wasn't with you." He joined her again. "You've been miles away since before we left the room."

She felt her face flush. "I know. I'm sorry."

"What's on your mind?"

"Nothing." She dropped her gaze to the ground. "Everything."

He worked his fingers into hers and started walking again. "Do you want to talk about it?"

"Not yet. I'm still not sure what I want to talk about."

"How about everything?"

She studied his profile, glad to see the slight smile that curved his lips. "Can we just enjoy the day? I don't want to ruin this grand surprise with my overly analytical thinking."

"I think that's a great idea."

His comment put her more at ease. He's not Thomas. She reminded herself. Wayne made it clear last night. Whatever she wanted to know, she needed only to ask. Maybe it was foolish of her to believe him, but until he gave her a reason not to, she refused to give into her self doubt.

Wayne walked them up the dirt path to the ranch where she'd gone horseback riding. "Why are we here?"

"Since you enjoyed your outing with Eric so much, I thought you might want to go for a horseback ride through the valley."

"I absolutely do not like horseback riding. They scare me."

He looked at her with a mixture of amusement and confusion. "Was there something else you had in mind?"

She shook her head. "I trust you."

"Good. And don't worry. I'll be here to catch you if you fall again."

Would he be so gentle with her heart?

Wayne made small talk with an older man. They got on their horses, and Val wasn't quite as stiff as she had been the day before. Wayne kept at her side, eyeing the horse to make sure it stayed on course next to him. They rode in silence for the first part of the trek, giving her a chance to admire the gorgeous scenery. She kept noticing new details she'd missed yesterday. Probably because she had been too nervous to give her surroundings much attention.

They came to a stop at a narrow river. The water was crystal clear, whispering past them toward the base of the valley. Wayne slid out of his saddle and helped her down. He motioned to a tall tree next to the river. A blanket and basket waited in the shade of the limbs.

She narrowed her eyes on him, but he ignored her and started unpacking the basket. After setting out two plates and cups, he motioned for her to join him.

"You are full of surprises, aren't you?"

He poured them both champagne. "I happened to know a guy."

She tucked her feet underneath her. "I'm still stuffed from breakfast."

He leaned over, brushing his lips against hers. "What were you thinking about earlier?"

She took a long swig of the bubbly drink, then rested the glass on top of her thigh. "I tend to think about the future. Like way into the future. It gives me a chance to play out possible scenarios of what could happen, and how it will affect my life, how I can change the outcome."

"I suppose one of those scenarios had something to do with us."

As she stared into his eyes, she glimpsed a future with him, and that sent a warmth through her chest. But she'd seen the same thing with Thomas. Thinking back on their relationship, she had intentionally ignored some red flags from the start.

"There you go again, wandering off without me."

She scrunched up her nose. "What if you change your mind about me; about us? You say you're okay with selling lemonade on the side of the road, but in reality, you are giving up a lot of income."

"How much money do you think I make as an escort?"

"I don't know. I'm not up on the current rate. It has to be substantial."

"Depends on what you consider substantial. It's not like I'm going on dates every night of the week. I try to keep it to a few times a month." He cocked his head to the side. "What about how our relationship will impact your life?"

Turning her eyes to the ground, she said, "Oh, yeah. It's totally going to clash with my long nights of sitting at home feeling sorry for myself. I mean, I can't imagine having to give up movie marathons and smashing whole pints of ice cream after a long day of work."

His laughter made her look up. "I would never ask you to give it up for me, but I'd totally be willing to give it a shot. To make you happy, of course."

They shared a round of laughter, ending with a tender kiss. When he leaned back, she turned her attention to where the horses grazed near the river.

"All jokes aside, I'd be lying if I said I wasn't scared. I came on this trip to rid myself of some heavy emotional baggage, not to find a relationship."

His smile never faltered. "I get it. That was the last thing on my mind as well. But I'm glad you showed up."

"Me too."

CHAPTER 30

WAYNE

WAYNE STOOD IN FRONT of the bathroom mirror, working the razor over his jaw in long, steady passes. His lips were curled into a silly smile. Val volunteered to help set things up for the rehearsal after running into Shiela when they returned to the resort. Despite the seriousness of their conversation, he felt like she was more at ease with her standing in his life. He wasn't naïve enough to think they weren't going to face hiccups while trying to navigate their new relationship, but he looked forward to facing those challenges with Val.

After making sure he'd gotten all the day-old stubble, he rinsed his face and went to the bedroom to finish dressing. In the living room, he grabbed his shoes, but a knock at the door distracted him.

He smiled, assuming it was Paul or his dad hiding from the wedding party. Shiela made it clear she and the other women knew exactly how they wanted things, and the men would only be in the way. It was an antiquated way of thinking in Wayne's opinion, but this was her wedding, and she had the last say.

"Coming," he called out.

He pulled open the door, about to grab his shoes, but the sight of Rita standing there made him step into the space of the door frame. "What the hell are you doing here? Have I not made myself crystal clear?"

Something about the self-satisfied smirk on her face made his skin go cold.

"You have. I'm here to give you a counteroffer."

Confused, he started to back away. "No thanks."

She held up a hand to keep him from closing the door.

"I said no. Now please, leave me—"

"I know about your little side business."

He froze. "A lot of people know about my photography."

Her laughter sounded sultry, but there was a menacing undertone. "The other business. The one where you sell yourself to women for money."

He pushed out a heavy laugh of his own. "I don't know what you're talking about. Leave me alone." Again, he tried to close the door, but she wouldn't budge.

"Dear, sweet, naughty Wayne. You really need to choose a different passcode for your phone."

His blood went cold. "You took my phone? When?"

"Last night, at the bar. You were plenty distracted after that heated conversation with Valerie. Where she blurted out your arrangement? Curious, I did a little digging and imagine my surprise when I found all those texts from those women begging you to please them. I knew I had to find proof if I am to convince you to hear me out, so I took screen shots and sent them to my email." She dropped the phone in his hand.

"And just what do you plan to do with this information? Blackmail me? Do you want me to pay you to keep quiet?"

Her laughter was like nails on a chalkboard to his frantic mind. "I don't need money."

"Then what is it you want from me?"

She worked her fingers up the front of his shirt, but he was too much in shock to move away. "Oh, Wayne. I just want you to give me a second chance. What I did was cowardly, but I felt so trapped. By the time I realized what a terrible mistake I made, you had already iced me out."

His throat constricted when she ran a long acrylic fingernail along his newly shaven jawline.

"I'd like the chance to prove how much I still care for you."

He finally broke free from the paralysis and took a step away from her. "Is that why you're threatening to expose me?"

"I'm willing to take this secret to my grave."

"For what price?"

She shrugged. "I want things the way it used to be. I want us to be the couple everyone envied."

"Too late for that. I'm with Val."

"So? You two don't seem that close."

"You're fucking crazy if you think I'm going to agree to this. Even if I did, I can't believe you would be okay living with someone who doesn't love you?"

She made a disgusted sound. "There's more to life than love. You and I made an amazing power couple. Your mom said as much, many times."

He had to force himself to unclench his jaw. "No." was all he could manage to say.

"You always were stubborn when it came to your morals. For once, would you think about the bigger picture? Do you know what kind of scandal this is going to cause when everyone finds out you are a male prostitute? Your dad will be a pariah in his firm. And your mom won't be able to show her face in public again."

Wayne thought she was being overly dramatic, but she wasn't far off the mark with his dad. Reputation was everything in his line of work.

"This is a lot to think about, so I'll extend the offer until after the wedding. It will give you time to let that sweet girl of yours down as cordially as you can. She seems the type to wilt easily."

Rita patted his cheek before lleaving.

Wayne stared dumbly at the door as it swung close. His first instinct was to go after Rita and tell her to shove her proposal up her snooty ass, but she had proof of his lifestyle. She could ruin him. Not only that, but she could also crush his entire family. He didn't want to even contemplate what would happen to Shiela and Paul if they got caught in the crossfire of the fallout.

The thought of betraying Val made him double over as if he'd been punched in the gut. He promised not to betray her like Thomas. No matter how many times he twisted and prodded his mind for a solution that wouldn't destroy the lives of those he loved, there was no happy ending for him or Val.

In the end, he had to choose between his and Val's happiness, or that of his family.

CHAPTER 31

VALERIE

As soon as Val spotted Wayne skulk into the venue, she knew something was off. His usual easygoing demeanor was now a pensive pucker on his tight features. Even more odd, he refused to look at her. Instead, he rounded the outer tables and going straight for the empty bar. He turned on the stool, facing away from the rest of the room.

Val stood at the end of the lineup of bridesmaids while Shiela and Jennifer argued about some trivial placement of flowers. No matter how hard Val stared at the back of Wayne's head, she couldn't mentally will him to turn her way. With the other women distracted, she took the opportunity to go to him.

He jumped at the feel of her hand running up his shoulder. "Hey." She kept her voice low and soothing. "Are you okay?"

His eyes swept over her, and she could tell his smile was forced. "I'm good."

"Did you find out what happened to your phone?"

That time he met her stare. "Yeah. I guess I misplaced it."

She tried to keep the worry off her face, but inside, her nerves were on fire. She wondered if he was having second thoughts about their relationship already? Before she hurdled herself down those dangerous lines of thought, she heard Shiela asking for everyone's attention.

"Since the guys are all here now, we can do a quick run through."

Wayne stood, gave Val a swift kiss on her cheek and went to stand with his future brother-in-law. She took up her place beside the other women, trying not to stare at him. For the rest of the rehearsal ceremony, she pretended to pay attention. She desperately searched her mind for Wayne's sudden change in character. She wanted to drag him outside, away from everyone else, and make him tell her what was going on.

Unfortunately, she never got the chance to be alone with him, because he never gave her an opportunity to get close enough to ask him to talk. Every time she started in his direction, he would get sucked into another chat with one family member or another. Had she not been an outsider, she might have barged in on their conversation.

As soon as the rehearsal was over, he all but ran for the lobby. Val politely excused herself from Sheila and the other bridesmaids so she could catch up to him. She didn't reach the elevator before it closed, so she tapped the call button, hissing for it to descend quicker. By the time she made it to the room, Wayne stood on the balcony, staring into the sky.

She took her time crossing the room, trying to calm herself. At the railing, she leaned forward, trying to catch his attention. "What is going on?"

"Nothing."

"Don't lie to me. I don't know what happened between this morning and now, but you are acting like a completely different person." She inched closer and drew his face to the side, so he had to look at her. "If you're having second thoughts, I want you to tell me."

His eyes glazed over with fresh tears. "I want nothing more than to be with you, Valerie. I promise. That's never changed."

"But something happened."

He went back to staring at the mountains. "I don't know what to do."

Val listened, as if she was in another person's body, when he confessed Rita had come by their suite. Val's chest squeezed tight around her lungs, making it hard to breathe. When he finished speaking, she stared at the space in front of them, her stomach twisting into tight knots. Her skin was slick with a clammy, frigid sweat.

When the silence became too much, she shook her head. "That's ridiculous. Surely, she doesn't expect you to agree to that kind of sham."

Again, he refused to look at her.

Val's stomach dropped. "Are you actually considering it?"

"You don't understand. If she exposes my past, it could devastate my entire family."

That much Val understood, but it still didn't make her any less furious that he'd be willing to live a life of misery just to avoid the unpleasant reality of his choices. Her body moved on its own, backing through the double doors.

"I'm so sorry, Val. I can't let my family, especially Sheila, suffer because of my stupid mistakes."

She braced herself against the flood of emotions threatening to drown her in her own misery. "Coward," she barked.

"I'm trying to do what's right."

She struggled to keep her lips pressed together, not wanting to give in to the tirade of bitter insults that begged to be unleashed. Despite the turmoil thundering through her blood, a quiet voice, the one who still hurt from what Thomas did, agreed with him. He had his family to think of.

And Val had her heart to protect.

Without another word, she went to her room and locked both doors. She grabbed the suitcase from the closet and hefted it onto the bed. Most of the clothes she packed earlier were still inside.

His knock was soft on the door. "Val, I'm so sorry."

She couldn't find the strength to push out the words she wanted to say, so she kept herself busy gathering her belongings. As soon as she zipped the suitcase, the reality of what she was about to do hit her like a punch in the gut. Sheila would be disappointed, sure, but Val had no other choice. She couldn't fake her way through the ceremony.

Once she had her bags packed, she grabbed the bridesmaid dress and opened the door. The rest of the suite sat quiet and empty. Relief and disappointment pressed in on her. Without giving herself a chance to rethink the decision, she rushed to the hall and down to the bride and groom's room. If she was lucky, Sheila would still be downstairs, and Val could simply drop the dress off at the front desk. Let Wayne explain to his sister why she was short a bridesmaid.

The door swung open to Paul, undoing his tie. The second he saw her tear-stained face, his smile dropped. "What happened? Is everything okay?"

Sheila appeared behind him. "What's going on?"

Val pushed the garment bag into Paul's chest. "I can't—" Her throat tightened, and she had to swallow back a sob. "I can't be in the wedding. I'm leaving. Tonight."

Shiela pulled Val into the room. "Did something happen between you and Wayne?"

Val tried to back away, but whatever hold she had on her emotions broke and a flood of tears fell down her cheeks. Sheila wrapped an arm around her shoulders, leading her farther into the suite before easing her onto the sofa. A few seconds later, a glass of cold water appeared in Val's hands. Sheila sat down beside her, holding a box of tissues.

After taking a long sip of the refreshing drink, Val said, "I'm sorry to do this to you at the last minute. I just can't—."

Shiela set the water on the coffee table in front of them. "I don't care about that. Tell me what happened."

Val didn't know where to start, or if she wanted to tell the truth. It wasn't her place to share Wayne's secret. Sucking in a calming breath, she said, "Wayne is getting back together with Rita." It was the closest to the truth she could admit.

Shiela turned her head to Paul, her mouth dropping open. Returning to Val, she said, "Are you sure? Did you overhear something? Did you see them together?"

Val shook her head. "He told me. He—" God, she just wanted to leave. "He doesn't want to, but she found out about…something and is using it to coerce him into taking her back."

Shiela relaxed into the couch. She took in a breath and let it out in a slow exhale. "This is about his escort business, isn't it?"

Val gaped at her, slack jawed. "You know?"

"I've known for a few months. A friend of a friend almost became one of his clients. I never told him because it's his life, his choice to live it however he wants. When I saw you two together, I thought things had changed."

Val closed her eyes. "We weren't together. Not at first." She told them about Lisa setting her up on the date, leaving out certain details of the night, as well as the subsequent series of unfortunate events leading to their arrangement. "He wanted a scapegoat to keep his mom off his back, and I needed a long overdue vacation."

Shiela stood and paced the length of the couch.

"I didn't mean to deceive you," Val said. "You were so kind to ask me to stand in as a bridesmaid—"

Shiela waved a hand. "It doesn't matter how things started between you." She sat down beside Val again. "What changed?"

Staring at nothing at all, Val said, "Somewhere along the way, we stopped pretending."

Sheila brushed a strand of hair out of her face. "Stay here with Paul. I need to make some phone calls."

Val stood with her. "I understand why he had to do this. As much as it hurts, I can't blame him."

"I'm sure he has good intentions, but I refuse to allow him to pave that road to hell for Rita." To Paul, she said, "I'll be back in a bit."

CHAPTER 32

WAYNE

"I'll have another." Wayne waved the empty glass at the bartender. He was working on his third scotch, but no matter how much he drank, the fiery alcohol couldn't burn away the guilt eating at his heart. The image of Val's anguished face still burned in his mind's eye and there was no one else to blame but him.

The bartender slid a fresh drink in front of him. Wayne gulped it down, grimacing at the bite in the back of his throat. His skin prickled with the warmth of the oncoming buzz, yet the memory of Valerie's tears and the pain in her voice remained at the forefront of his thoughts.

There was no universe where he would actually go through with Rita's demands. It didn't matter the fallout. He couldn't bear the thought of living in a loveless relationship for the rest of his life. But he was too late to make things right with Val. She deserved better. Someone who had the strength to fight for her heart. Not some coward that hid behind a false sense of duty to a family he didn't even want to be a part of.

After their conversation in the valley, he began to wonder if he would be able to provide a life for them on his amateur photographer's salary. He hadn't been truthful with her about just how much money he made as an escort. In the beginning, he played with the idea of upping his clientele because the money was so good. He'd never make a living wage on his meager earnings shooting one or two weddings a year. And he cared too much for Val to enmesh her further into his family dynamics.

Maybe he should accept his uncle's proposal. It would give Wayne the means to make some kind of life for them. It also meant Val would have to sacrifice the life she built in New Mexico. In the end, when faced with the decision, he took the path of least resistance. He let her go.

"I am going to burn your family's name to the ground."

Wayne's head came around to the sound of his sister's voice. He could count on one hand how many times he'd heard her so angry. Rita came around the corner of the bar, spotted Wayne, and rushed to his side.

"You better control your sister, or I will make sure your whole family is ruined."

The fire in Sheila's eyes matched the venom in her voice. "You want ruin? I'll give you ruin."

Wayne got up from the barstool when Rita slid in behind him. "What the hell is going on?" His legs weren't so steady, given the three drinks he'd just downed.

"Move out of the way," Shiela demanded. "I should have done this a long time ago."

Rita shoved a manicured nail past his shoulder. "I don't know what you think you have on my family, but—"

"I know everything," Sheila spat. "You're not the only one with connections. Check your email. Go on. The first document is a gift."

Wayne felt Rita shift at his back. He turned around and watched her flip through the phone. The color drained from her face, and she looked like she was going to throw up.

"How did you get this?"

"Doesn't matter. I want you to understand just how screwed you are if you don't drop this whole charade with my brother. Whatever you think you know about him, I can promise it's nowhere near as damning as the information I have access to."

Rita fought to put her mask back in place. She pushed the button on the side of the phone, making the screen go black.

Refusing to look at Wayne, she brushed past him to stand in front of Shiela. "When I find out how you got this—"

"Shove it, Rita." Shiela held out her hand. "Give me your phone."

Rita drew the device into her body. "Absolutely not."

"Unlock it and hand it over. I'm going to make sure you don't have anything unseemly tucked away in there." When Rita still didn't give it over, Shiela took out her own phone and held it up, ready to dial. "One call. That's all I need to bury your world in scandal."

Rita practically shoved her phone in Shiela's outstretched hand. His sister moved fast, scrolling through the phone. When she was done, she pushed it into Rita's waiting fingers. "I really hate you won't be able to attend my wedding. I understand you have other pressing matters to see to. Oh, and say hi to your daddy for me."

Wayne shook himself out of the alcoholic stupor, gaping at the woman he barely recognized. Before he could speak, Sheila snatched him by the arm.

"And you," The anger in her eyes softened. "God, you're such an idiot."

"What just happened?" The floaty feeling in his head made it hard for him to concentrate on coherent thought.

"Great, you're drunk. Oh well, she's already seen you at your worst."

He snatched his arm out of her grasp. "What are you talking about? What did you do?"

"Once again, I have to save your ass. I swear. You can be so oblivious to the world around you." She grabbed his arm again, less forcefully than before. "Come on."

CHAPTER 33

VALERIE

"Val, are you okay?"

The sound of Shiela's voice shook Val out of a daze. Her eyes burned from crying so much. It took her a while to finally numb herself to the pain in her chest. She blotted her face with a hand towel and opened the door. "I'm fine. I should grab my things and go."

"You're not going anywhere."

Her lungs constricted, but she forced a smile. "I can't stay."

Shiela stepped away from the door, letting her by. Val came around the corner of the living area to be confronted by Wayne sitting at the table, nursing a cup of coffee. He glanced up and when he saw her, he was on his feet. Before she could react, his arms engulfed her in a hug so tight she had to take shallow breaths.

"Val, I'm so sorry." His warm breath against her ear sent shivers down her spine.

The temptation to give into the embrace, to forgive him, was so strong. She unclenched her hands and started to reach around him. But her heart hurt too much. She pushed away from him. "No. You don't get to do that. You can't just say you're sorry and expect everything to be okay."

"I know. I was scared. I didn't think I was enough for you. That I can't give you the life you deserved."

"Do you honestly believe I'm so shallow?"

"Of course not." His lips trembled. "I've never met anyone like you. I'm used to people fixated on status and appearance, whereas you care more about integrity and honesty. And I've let you down in both regards."

Had he let her down, though? Val tried to hang on to her anger, but if she had been in the same situation, no matter how crazy her family tended to be, she would have done everything in her power not to hurt them. Not when her parents had proven how much they were willing to sacrifice for her. Family was sometimes complicated like that.

Val stepped around him. "Shiela, if Rita exposes Wayne, how bad is it going to affect you?"

"Oh, she won't be doing that."

"How can you be so sure?"

Shiela smiled, and it reminded her of a cat cornering its prey. "Apparently, Wayne forgot I've known Rita and her family since I was in middle school. I even dated her cousin in college. I became privy to a lot of their dirty little secrets. One of which is how much her daddy likes pretty, young college girls." She eyed Wayne. "As tempting as it was to play that hand when Rita left you, I was glad she was out of our lives."

To Val, she said, "Even if I didn't have the means to stop her from telling everyone the truth, I wouldn't care. And neither would our dad. As for Jennifer, I honestly couldn't care less what happens to her."

Wayne frowned at his sister.

"Don't give me that look. I only put up with her because of you and dad. You know how insufferable she is."

His expression relaxed. "She's still my mom."

"And you will always be my baby brother. I may not be able to stop you from making questionable choices, but I'll always be here to help you out of trouble." She scrunched up her nose. "Unless you deserve it."

Paul came forward, wrapping an arm around Shiela's waist. He watched his future wife with a mixture of awe and trepidation. "Remind me never to get on your bad side."

Wayne cupped Val's face in his hand. "Will you at least agree to talk? Just you and I?"

Val looked from Wayne to Sheila. All she wanted to do was get away from those piercing stares. "Okay."

Wayne's presence stayed at her back the entire walk to their suite. Once they were in their room and the door closed, he said, "I don't know where to start."

She whirled on him. "Let me make one thing clear, Wayne Mc-Nab. Whatever we are; were, it ended the moment you decided to choose Rita over us."

He reached for her, but she batted his hand away. "I gave you every opportunity to be honest and up front with me." A ball of anger and pain lodged in the back of her throat, and she had to take in a long, ragged breath before she could go on.

"Here is what's going to happen. You and I will pretend we made up and everything is good between us. God knows your sister doesn't need any more drama at her wedding. We are going back to the status quo. When the wedding is over, I'll go home. Alone. Where we won't see or talk to each other ever again."

Even with her vision blurred from tears, she could see the devastation pulling at Wayne's face. His eyes glistened with the same sadness running rampant inside her. "Please don't do this. I swear I never meant to hurt you."

His words tore at her resolve. "And what happens when you get scared again. What if Rita tries to win you back? What if you decide monogamy isn't what you really want? I can't go through this again. I won't."

He stood there, staring at her in silence for what seemed like eons. Finally, he closed his eyes and nodded. "I understand. We'll make it through the wedding, and I'll be out of your life."

On the outside, she appeared calm, but on the inside, she begged herself not to let it end like this. Now, it was her turn to play the coward. So, she whirled around and went to the bedroom, locking it behind her. On the bed, she was hit by the scent of his cologne, and it took every ounce of strength not to break down and scream.

Her anger toward Wayne was overshadowed by the frustration gnawing at her insides because she understood why he chose the path he did. Yet it didn't lessen the anguish she felt. It only made her decision to shut him out that much harder.

CHAPTER 34

WAYNE

WAYNE WAITED UNTIL HE heard Val leave the bathroom before dragging himself off the couch. He didn't bother unfolding the hide-a-bed before laying down the night before. Nor did he get much sleep. For hours, he stared at the ceiling, frantically thinking of a way to undo the damage he caused. If he hadn't been so scared of letting himself feel again; if he wasn't so consumed by the inherent financial bias his family instilled in him, maybe he would have trusted himself to believe Val wasn't as superficial as most of the people in his life.

Staring into the mirror, the man looking back disgusted him. A scared man, willing to destroy the trust of a woman he cared so deeply for. Even after only a handful of days of getting to know Val, there was no one else who would ever compare to her. The realization cut him deeper than the callousness of her words last night.

Pushing away from the sink, he got into the shower. After draying off, he remembered his clothes were in the bedroom. Wrapping the towel around his waist, he knocked at the shared door between the bathroom and bedroom. "I need to grab some clothes."

No answer.

He pulled the door open just enough to peek out. The room was empty. Val's suitcase sat on the edge of the bed, open and full of her things. No doubt as soon as the wedding was over, she'd come back and finish packing so she could make a hasty exit. Maybe this was for the best. She deserved so much better. She deserved to be with someone who gave her the trust and commitment she had been so willing to give him.

Once he finished dressing, he headed downstairs to where the other groomsmen had their own area to get dressed. He was tempted to take a detour to the bar for a quick shot of something strong and numbing, but this was his sister's special day. He needed to be sober and clear-headed to watch her marry the man of her dreams. And he wanted the chance to imprint Valerie in his memory one last time.

It was hard, putting on a smile when he entered the room with the other guys. They laughed at something Paul said, and when he spotted Wayne, he nodded to a hanging bag near a full-length mirror. "I thought I was going to have to send someone to drag your butt down here. Your suit is over there."

"I didn't get much sleep."

The others shared a look and chuckled at each other. Wayne wasn't about to tell them it wasn't like that, but he agreed with Val when it came to making this wedding perfect for Sheila. "Get your heads out of the gutter," he muttered, snatching the bag from the hanger.

He tried to adjust his tie when he spotted Paul heading his way. "How did it go?"

Wanting to keep the promise he made, Wayne smiled. "I think we are going to be okay."

Paul's grin widened. "I'm glad to hear it."

Wayne turned his attention to the mirror where he took too long getting his tie just right. A pang of sadness rose in his chest, wishing he could find Val and have her tie it for him again. He loved to watch her face when she concentrated.

When he was dressed, he excused himself from the room and took a walk around the garden. He needed some time alone to compose himself for what was going to be the hardest day of his life. On the one hand, he was excited and happy for Sheila, but on the other, he knew once the ceremony ended, he would probably never see Val again. And there was nothing he could think to say or do to keep her from walking out on him forever.

CHAPTER 35

VALERIE

VAL STARED IN THE mirror, running a hand down the delicate fabric of the bridesmaid's dress. In the background, there was a buzz of excited chatter from Sheila and the other girls. Val was glad they were distracted and not focused on her. She didn't want to do anything else to ruin Sheila's day.

Movement outside the window to her right drew her attention to the garden. Her heart stuttered inside her chest when she saw Wayne come into view. The sight of him chipped away at her wavering resolve. Despite what she told him the night before, in her heart, she wanted nothing more than to forget the last twenty-four hours and go back to the tentative relationship they just started to explore. But she was so scared of being hurt again.

A presence appeared at her back. When Val turned, Sheila held out a small gift bag.

"What's this?"

Sheila pushed it into Val's hands. "A little something from me, to show you just how much I appreciate stepping into this role." Her eyes went to the window. "You didn't have to pretend to stay together on my behalf."

Val felt a rush of heat run up her neck and face. "I—"

Sheila cut her off by stepping in front of her and the window. "I can tell when he's trying to fake being happy. You are allowed to feel angry, hurt, and betrayed. What Wayne did was probably the most moronic thing I've ever witnessed in his entire life. I realize you haven't known him all that long, but we can both agree he doesn't have the best track record of decision making."

Val looked away.

Sheila put her hands on Val's shoulders. "Except when he asked you to stay. It doesn't matter how you met. I know my brother, and I haven't seen him this happy in years. Not even when he was with Rita."

Val frowned. If Wayne had been so unhappy with her, then why had he been so eager to turn Val away to appease people who made him miserable? "I'm not sure I can trust him again."

Sheila nodded. "I'm not trying to convince you to decide one way or the other. I just want you to know you aren't the only one that's scared to love again." She left Val alone, returning to her friends.

Val glanced outside, but Wayne was already gone. Her heart begged her to go to him, but her head refused to let her legs carry her there.

From inside the beautiful packaging, she pulled out a simple pearl necklace. The silver chain draped over her fingers, delicate and lovely. After putting on the necklace, she went to the mirror, hoping she could at least pretend to be happy.

When it was time for the ceremony, Val's stomach twisted into a tight ball. She was last in line to walk up the aisle, preparing the way for Sheila. The second she stepped through the open double doors, all eyes were on her, but there was only one set making her heart flutter. Wayne's gaze followed her for the entire walk to the altar. Though his expression appeared stoic to anyone else, she saw the shift in his demeanor the closer she got to him. His chest rose and his nostrils flared like they did when he made love to her. Every step brought her closer to a decision she thought she was ready to make.

She tried to focus on the ceremony, fighting a losing battle of ignoring those piercing eyes locked on her. Every word spoken filtered through her brain like a fog of indecipherable language until the real world crashed into her when Sheila and Paul were pronounced man and wife.

Val blinked a few times to clear her mangled thoughts and followed the bride and groom down the aisle, where they would meet up again at the reception.

For a long time, she stood just outside the pavilion, a bystander, watching everyone mingle with each other. She didn't belong there, but when she turned to leave, Sheila swept by her.

"The party is this way."

Forcing a smile, Val pushed aside her insecurity, telling herself it was only a couple of more hours. Then she'd be free to go back home. But in the back of her mind, she already mourned the loss of what was never meant to be.

She kept to the periphery of the celebration, hoping to be ignored. What she didn't expect was the hand slipping into hers. Wayne stepped in front of her, his expression hopeful.

"Would you like to dance?"

Unable to stop herself, she smiled. "I'd love to."

The world spun around as he took her onto the dance floor. No matter how badly she wanted to hate being so close to Wayne, the feel of his body next to hers was intoxicating. He tucked her hands against his chest, resting his lips against her ear. "I've come to terms with your decision. There's nothing I can say or do to change the past." His voice cracked, and it took him a few seconds to continue. "When you showed up, I never imagine how quickly I'd fall in love with you."

She tensed, stopping them in the middle of the other couples swaying around them. Her vision blurred, and a fierce tremor of anger tempered with excitement and fear made her heart race. How dare he say those words. They weren't real. Other people didn't fall in love so quickly. Not like she did.

He leaned back, resting his hands on the sides of her face. "I want you to find the happiness you deserve. I only wish I could be the one to give it to you."

Her eyes darted back and forth, looking over the room full of strangers. She had to get out of there. The world closed in around her and she found it difficult to breathe. Wayne tried to hold on to her, but she slipped out of his grasp and managed to reach the lobby before he caught up to her.

"Valerie, wait."

She stood in front of the elevator, hitting the call button in a futile attempt to make it descend faster. "I can't do this." Her voice quivered with emotion.

He stepped into view, his face mirroring the concern in his voice. "I meant what I said."

She glared at him. "How can you?" Then walked around him toward the door to the stairwell, but he followed after. Speaking more to herself than Wayne, she said, "How can you love me when we barely know each other?" She stopped herself before she admitted she felt the same way.

Her footsteps echoed on the stone steps and when she got to the first landing, she glanced back to where Wayne stood on the first step.

"I think I started to fall in love with you on our first night together."

The confession made her grip the railing, halting her ascent.

He took another step. "For the first time in a very long time, I could be myself. Everything I said to you is the truth. Every story. Every fear and desire. I've never felt so comfortable around a complete stranger."

Val shook her head, blinking away tears. "But it was all based on a lie. Even here. We've been lying to everyone. Especially ourselves. How do you know that your feelings aren't just as fake?"

He made two more steps. "I love you, Valerie Peters. There's nothing more concrete and real in my life than what I feel for you right now."

She turned, focusing on the stairs, promising to take her back to the room where she could finally escape this charade. But no matter how hard she tried, her hands wouldn't let go of the railing. "Did you love me when you agreed to go back to Rita?"

After a long pause, he said, "Yes. I was scared you couldn't love me back. After everything I've done, the life I made for myself, how could anyone ever love something so tainted and broken?"

Unable to stop herself, Val laughed. She covered her mouth, fighting off a sob. "You can be really dense, you know that?"

Confusion took the place of devastation.

When she met his stare, her lips trembled at the fear of the confession about to pass over her tongue. "I'm a nobody, Wayne. Just some boring woman stuck in a boring career, living a boring life."

He opened his mouth, but she cut him off.

"Then I met you. Do you want to know the real reason I went home with you that night?" Her cheeks reddened at the thought of confessing the truth. "You were the first man to make me believe in love at first sight. When I found out the truth about you, it crushed me to my soul. I convinced myself you were simply playing a part Lisa paid for. And as stupid as it sounds, when I ran into you again, I thought maybe the universe knew better. Turns out it did."

He made the short trek up the stairs until he was eye to eye with her. His hands were balled into fists around the bottom of his jacket, as if to keep himself grounded. "Please don't walk away from us."

She considered his words, her heart waging war with her head. In the end, both logic and emotion came to the same conclusion. "I'm scared."

"Me too, Val. But I don't want to let fear dictate the rest of my life."

Again, she looked upward. There was no hiding her heart anymore. Wayne had already taken possession of it. When their eyes met again, she knew there was no going back. No matter how things turned out, now, in this moment, she loved him.

She slid her hand down the railing, covering his. "Of course I'll stay," she whispered.

He drew her into his arms, his lips caressing hers. Their moment of happiness was interrupted by the door being pushed open.

"There you are."

Val glanced down to find Melissa leaning inside the stairwell. "The bride and groom are about to leave and want everyone present for the bouquet toss."

"We will be right there," Wayne said. When they were alone, he took a handkerchief from his pocket and dabbed at Val's eyes. "We don't want to disappoint my sister."

Before he turned away, she grabbed onto the lapel of his suit jacket, kissing him again. "I love you too."

A Word from the Author

At its core, *Imperfect Illusions* is a story about masks—the ones we wear for others, the ones we wear for ourselves, and the truths we try to bury beneath them. It's about love in its rawest form, tangled with regret, longing, and the fear of being truly seen.

Writing this book was an exploration of vulnerability—of how easy it is to build walls and how terrifying it can be to let someone in. Wayne and Val's journey isn't perfect, but that's what makes it real. Love is messy, uncertain, and often wrapped in illusions we don't even realize we're creating.

To those who have ever questioned their own worth, who have struggled with choices they can't take back, or who have longed for something just out of reach—this story is for you.

Thank you for taking this journey with me. I hope *Imperfect Illusions* resonates with you in some way, whether it's a whisper of recognition or a reminder that even the most broken pieces can still find their way back together.

With gratitude,
C. A. Hollister

Also available by C. A. Hollister

Destiny Unbound: Laws of Fate Book 1